FALLING FOR
HIS CONVENIENT
QUEEN

WA

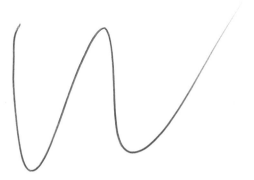

FALLING FOR HIS CONVENIENT QUEEN

THERESE BEHARRIE

MILLS & BOON

First published in Great Britain 2018
by Mills & Boon, an imprint of HarperCollins*Publishers*
1 London Bridge Street, London, SE1 9GF

Large Print edition 2018

© 2018 Therese Beharrie

ISBN: 978-0-263-07385-0

MIX
Paper from
responsible sources
FSC® C007454

This book is produced from independently certified
FSC™ paper to ensure responsible forest management.
For more information visit www.harpercollins.co.uk/green.

Printed and bound in Great Britain
by CPI Group (UK) Ltd, Croydon, CR0 4YY

For my husband, who so graciously told me
I could dedicate my books to other people
sometimes, too. You're my best friend, babe.
This is your life now.

And for my father. Thank you
for all you've done to get me here.

I love you both.

CHAPTER ONE

THIS WASN'T A MISTAKE. This wasn't a mistake.

Princess Nalini of Mattan repeated the words to herself as she watched the castle she'd called home for the last twenty-six years fade into the distance. With a sick feeling in her stomach, she forced herself to look ahead.

The place that would become her new home—the castle of Kirtida—grew clearer as the boat she was on drew nearer. It was a large ominous-looking building that had her heart jumping and her mind replaying those reassuring words again.

'We're almost there,' Zacchaeus's voice sounded in her ear, and she shivered. It was as much because of the brisk sea air as it was the proximity of the man she was engaged to.

King Zacchaeus of Kirtida.

Mattan had been in an alliance with Kirtida and a third kingdom, Aidara, for centuries. It was called the Alliance of the Three Isles, and up until Zacchaeus had overthrown his father a few months ago, the three islands along the coast of South Africa had been united and strong.

Though there'd been a general concern about Zacchaeus's actions, it had only grown alarming when Zacchaeus had refused communication with Mattan and Aidara after the coup. And then he hadn't attended the State Banquet meant to affirm the alliance between the isles, and that alarm had spurred Nalini's brother, King Xavier of Mattan, and the Queen of Aidara, Leyna, into action. They'd announced their engagement and a day later Zacchaeus had made contact.

Which was the reason *she* was currently on her way to a new home.

She angled towards him, and felt guilt hit her almost as hard as the attraction did.

His hair was dark, complementing the caramel of his skin and the slight stubble on his jaw. The lines of his face were serious, intense, and strikingly carved. If she hadn't been intimidated by the clothing he'd chosen to wear—all black, and a clear show of power—she *definitely* would have been intimidated by his looks. Or, worse still, by the *pull* to that power. By the pull to those looks.

But she couldn't ignore the guilt.

She couldn't be attracted to this man. It couldn't matter that his shirtsleeves were rolled up muscular arms, or that his trousers were perfectly moulded to powerful legs. Not when Zacchaeus had demanded that Nalini marry him before he would sign the papers affirming Kirtida's place in the alliance.

And until those papers were signed her kingdom would be in danger.

'I've had a meal prepared for us,' Zacchaeus said as they arrived at Kirtida. He jumped off the boat and offered her a hand. She hesitated but took it, her lungs tightening at the unease that crept up her arm at the contact.

Because it *was* unease. The dull throb that had started when he'd touched her. The flash of heat. It *was* unease, she told herself again, but couldn't bring herself to look at him.

'I assume you're hungry?'

'You wouldn't have to assume if you'd asked,' she replied lightly, shaking off her discomfort. She'd made the choice to come to Kirtida. She'd chosen to save her kingdom by marrying Zacchaeus. The time to choose was over and, because of that, she needed to be civil with him. 'But I'd love to eat something, thank you.'

Zacchaeus nodded and, after instructing that Nalini's things be taken to the room she'd be staying in while they planned their wedding, told her to follow him. Goosebumps shot out on her skin as she entered the castle, but she straightened her shoulders.

The interior was a beautiful combination of old and new, its stone pillars rich with history and its wooden floors in a modern style.

He stopped in front of a room with a large dining table and, wordlessly, stepped aside for her to pass. As she did, the staff scattered to accommodate her at the table and, before she knew it, she was seated next to Zacchaeus. She waited a moment and then asked, 'Is anyone else joining us?'

A shadow crossed over his face. 'No.'

She nodded and then forced herself to ask her next question. 'Your parents…are they… Do they still live here?'

The shadow darkened, and Nalini braced for

him to tell her to mind her own business. But a few seconds later his face settled into a blank expression, and his brown eyes—a combination of honey and cinnamon that contrasted with the dark features of his face—met hers.

'They're still here, yes. I haven't banished them, if that's what you're thinking.'

'I'm not quite sure what to think, to be honest. I'm not familiar with what happens after a coup.'

Something flickered in his eyes and her stomach dipped. She shouldn't have said it, she thought, but if she didn't… Well, she didn't want to spend the rest of her life biting her tongue. Or falling in line just because she'd been told to. Coming to Kirtida had been a way to escape that life. She wasn't simply going to settle for another version of it.

'They live on the royal property,' Zacchaeus said, interrupting her thoughts. 'Not in the castle.'

'Will I see them?'

'I'm not sure,' he said impassively. 'There might not be enough time before the wedding.'

'Planning this wedding is going to take some time.'

'I'm sure it will.' He paused. 'But let's not pretend that you only want that time to plan a wedding.'

'What do you mean?'

He lifted an eyebrow. 'I know that you're also here because you—or, more specifically, your family—want to know whether I really intend on signing the papers to confirm Kirtida's place in the alliance.'

She told herself not to gape. Forced herself not to ask how he knew. Instead, she went for honesty. 'You're right. Except it's *me* who wants to know. *I'm* the one marrying you to ensure that you sign.'

'You have my word,' he said, and she heard the sincerity in his tone. 'Once Xavier, Leyna and I come to an agreement about the Protection of the Alliance of the Three Isles clause, you and I will marry and I'll sign those papers.'

'And if I don't believe you?' she asked softly, compelled by the voice in her head that warned her against trusting so easily. The voice that she'd ignored when she'd been younger.

'That's why you're here, isn't it?' he replied. 'To figure out whether you can?' She nodded mutely. 'Do that, then.'

The food began to arrive as he said the words, and she was relieved that she wouldn't have to come up with a reply she didn't have. But the servers did their work quickly and, before she knew it, she and Zacchaeus were alone again.

'Your family,' he said, reaching for the glass that held his wine. 'They didn't have anything to say about your plan? To organise the wedding from Kirtida and figure out whether you could trust me?'

She almost told him the truth. But that would have entailed admitting the displeasure of her mother and grandmother at her decision. It would have meant telling him about how they thought that she was being reckless—a description they'd used for her for the past nine years, despite her efforts to change that perception. How even her brother had thought that, and how she'd expected more of him.

No, the truth included a myriad of things that she didn't want to think about, let alone tell *him*.

'It made sense,' she said instead. 'Since, as we discussed over the phone, the wedding will be here, planning it on Kirtida was the logical decision.'

'And you always make logical decisions?'

'Does marrying a man I barely know sound logical?'

He smiled a slow, crooked smile that made him look even more dangerous. 'Reasonable, then.'

'It's not reasonable either. Not for a normal person, anyway. But we're not normal and so, in that sense, this is *both* logical and reasonable.' She paused. 'I also know your people have responded positively to the news of our engagement. So, if I'm here and they see their future Queen plan a wedding with their King, it could strengthen their support of this marriage.'

There was an uneasy silence after her words, and she frowned. 'You don't agree with me?'

'So you told your family this and they agreed to let you come here?' he asked, not answering her question.

The uneasiness began to swirl in her chest.

'You're wondering whether my brother sent me,' she replied, ignoring the feeling. 'He didn't. He wasn't entirely happy with this decision.'

'Because he worried that I would find out why you were really here?'

Because he still sees me as an irresponsible teenager.

'Why would he worry that you'd find out I wanted to know if we could trust you? There's a reason you figured it out so quickly, Zacchaeus. It wasn't meant to be some great secret.'

'Why didn't he want you to come then?'

'Probably because he wouldn't be able to protect me.' She nearly rolled her eyes.

'He thought you needed to be protected? From me?' Unhappiness flashed across his face.

'Do you blame him? You forced him to choose between protecting his baby sister and protecting his kingdom.'

'But he chose his kingdom.'

'No, *I* chose *our* kingdom.' She watched him carefully, and wondered at the emotion she couldn't quite read on his face. 'Xavier didn't want me to do this. Not as a king, but as a brother. He didn't want to have his sister marry a man he wasn't sure he could trust. So when I told him I would come here, plan the wedding and see whether we *could* trust you, he didn't like it, but he understood.' And because it seemed as if he needed to hear it, she repeated, 'This was *my* choice, Zacchaeus.'

'Why? Why would you choose to marry a man you barely know?'

She frowned at the rush of answers that came to mind, none of which was appropriate to tell him. 'You didn't *really* give us a choice. Your actions over the past few months have shown us exactly what you're capable of. So when I said I chose this, I just meant that it wasn't Xavier who did. There is no real choice when it comes to protecting our kingdoms, is there?'

She watched a stony expression settle on his face and felt her frown deepen. He looked so unhappy at everything she'd just said. As though it was news to him. As though *he* wasn't the one who'd started—*forced*—it all.

'You're right, there isn't,' he answered her quietly. 'Which is why we're in this situation in the first place.'

'Because Macoa threatened Kirtida with sanctions?'

He nodded. She waited for an explanation to follow—any explanation, really, as to why an ally of Kirtida and the alliance had suddenly made threats after years of working together peacefully.

'Why?' she asked when he didn't continue. 'I mean, I know that's why you want the alliance's Protection clause updated before we get married. Before you sign to reaffirm the alliance between our kingdoms. You want protection against international allies like Macoa to be included in the agreement too. But *why* do you need that protection? Since—' she hesitated, and then forced herself to say it '—since I'm going to be your wife, I'd like to know.'

'It's complicated,' he said simply. Darkly.

'I'm going to be Queen to your people, Zacchaeus. Don't you think that's enough to share details about complicated matters with me?'

'You're not Queen yet,' he replied. 'And when you are I'll tell you what you need to know.'

'What you *think* I need to know, maybe.' She clenched her jaw and then forced herself to relax. 'The least you could do is tell me why I'm here.'

'You know why you're here, Nalini.' His eyes were sombre. 'Without our marriage, there's no guarantee that Kirtida's place in the alliance won't be undermined by Leyna and Xavier's marriage. By the bond that that will create between Mattan and Aidara.'

'I'd like to know the *real* reason. The one that had you calling us after you found out Kirtida might not be protected as well as Mattan and Aidara were if Leyna and Xavier married.'

Again, silence followed her words. This time she couldn't help the muscles that tightened in her shoulders.

'There's still no guarantee, you know,' she reminded him. 'There won't be until you sign the papers affirming Kirtida's place in the alliance.'

'And you know my conditions for doing that. After the negotiations to protect our kingdoms. After our marriage.' He tilted his head. 'Are you hoping I'd tell you I'd sign before either are in place?'

'Of course not.' But there *had* been a part of her that had hoped for exactly that.

'So you're not looking for a loophole? You haven't realised that you've made a mistake after this conversation with me?' He leaned forward, making her briefly notice the food they'd otherwise forgotten. 'You don't want to return to the safety of Mattan?'

'I'm safe here,' she said, her eyes darting towards the door where her Mattanian guards—who would continue protecting her as Queen of Kirtida—stood.

'That wasn't what I meant.'

'I know.' She fell silent. 'I think this will work best if you just say what you mean, Zacchaeus, and don't expect me to guess.'

He nodded and met her gaze. 'I'm not going to change my mind, Nalini. You're going to marry me.'

She didn't look away. Though the trembling that had gone through her heart at his words made her want to, she didn't. This was her life now. And this life had been *her* choice.

She thought of the teenage girl who had once been so filled with hope. Who'd thought that taking a chance on a boy would finally bring her the freedom she'd craved. She thought about the girl who'd had that hope dashed so quickly—so heartbreakingly—that she hadn't wanted to make another decision for herself since.

Until now.

Nalini reminded herself of that. She wasn't the girl who hoped for love or sought freedom any more. Who rebelled and made stupid mistakes. But that was still how her family saw her. The mistake she'd made when she was a teen had completely changed their view of her. More importantly, it had changed *her* view of herself.

When she'd told Xavier she would marry Zacchaeus, she'd seen it as a chance to make up for that mistake. To prove to herself and to her family that she was *more*.

Considering their reactions to her decision, she knew she hadn't succeeded in making them believe that yet. But if she stayed—if she went through with this marriage—she would be saving her kingdom. Her family would have no choice *but* to see her as responsible.

And she could finally, *finally* stop trying to convince them that she was.

'In that case, I suppose this time is even more important for us, isn't it?'

CHAPTER TWO

'WHAT DO YOU MEAN?' Zacchaeus asked his fiancée, watching her closely. 'I thought this was already important.'

'That's why I said *even more* important,' she answered brightly. 'Since we're going to be married, we should use this time to build a foundation for this marriage. Preferably one of mutual respect.'

He didn't answer. It was the second time she'd said something about the two of them spending time together. Getting to know one another. But, just as he had the first time, he brushed it off. There would be none of that.

Even if he *was* fascinated by her.

She'd covered it up quickly, but Zacchaeus knew that there was something more to what she'd just said. Something that proved his suspicions that she wasn't just marrying him to protect her kingdom. Which would make complete sense. She *was* sacrificing her entire future for Mattan. Would she really do that without having some other motive?

And yet, since that was exactly what *he* was doing, why couldn't she?

'Do you agree?' she asked, her eyes steady on his.

He got caught in them for a moment, and almost found himself telling her that he did. But he stopped himself. Forced himself to focus. Reminded himself that just because those blue-grey eyes, those full pink lips, those dark curls with its light streaks, painted a picture he couldn't bring himself to stop looking at—had never been able to—didn't mean he should forget why she was there.

He'd already told her too much. Like the fact that his parents—or rather his father—still lived on royal property. He'd panicked when she'd asked about seeing them, though he was sure he'd answered her without letting her know how much her question had alarmed him.

Because when she'd asked he'd pictured her seeing his father and realising the former King of Kirtida was ill. He'd pictured her asking about his mother and finding out that the Queen had left over two months ago. That somehow she'd learn about how the coup had been staged because of his father's ill health and that the threat against his kingdom was his mother's fault.

No, he couldn't afford to be distracted by how beautiful she was or by the bright light she carried within her. So he would remind them both of why she was there—and it wasn't to get to know one another.

'I agree that our marriage is important.' He paused so that his next words would have the impact he needed for her to understand. 'For the sake of our kingdoms.'

'But not for our relationship?'

'We don't have to have a relationship to be married.'

His parents had proved that to him, hadn't they?

But the silence that followed his words told him that she wasn't happy with his answer. And the longer he waited for one from her, the more the tension grew between them. He remembered for the first time then that they were supposed to be eating. But he couldn't even distract himself by doing that since he knew that their food had gone cold.

'What will the next few weeks look like for us then?' she asked eventually, breaking the silence.

'Well, you're here under the pretence of planning our wedding, so you should probably do that.'

'Alone?'

'Yes.'

'And what will you be doing?'

'Negotiating the Protection clause with your brother and future sister-in-law.'

There was a pause. And then she asked, 'So you expect me to spend all my time planning a wedding?'

'I've already given you my word that I'll sign the documents when the time comes, Nalini. The other reason you're here isn't really necessary.'

'And I'm just supposed to believe you?'

'Yes.'

'Why can't you do the same then? Believe that I'll marry you after the papers are signed, I mean.'

'Because there's more on the line for me. This is my entire kingdom.' And what was left of his family, he thought, his throat tightening. 'I can't just take your word on it.'

She stared at him. 'Do you hear yourself? Do you hear the hypocrisy in what you're saying?'

He shrugged as though her words didn't affect him. '*You* agreed to the terms of *this* situation, Nalini. We haven't discussed the one you're proposing now, and I haven't agreed to it.'

Her eyes flashed, making them more grey than blue, and he felt a dangerous—and unwanted—tug of attraction. 'So not only do you expect me to accept that you'll do as you say, but you also won't even give me a chance to figure out whether I can trust that you will?'

'What would change if you realised you couldn't trust me? Would you return to Mattan?'

Something flickered in her eyes. 'It would change things.'

'Would it? So you'd tell Xavier and Leyna that you can't go through with the wedding and put the entire alliance at risk?'

'It's interesting how you've turned this around. How you've made risking the alliance sound like it isn't something *you've* been doing from the moment you refused to see Xavier and Leyna after you became King.' She leaned forward. 'Like you aren't holding us hostage now and *still* doing it.'

She was right. But he couldn't afford to think of it that way. If he did, he'd have to pay heed to the emotions circling inside him like sharks around prey. He couldn't allow them to attack. Not when the threat of them had been propelling him forward, helping him to focus on what Kirtida needed.

He'd been telling the truth when he'd told her he had more on the line than she did. He'd somehow managed to convince Xavier and Leyna that they needed him just as much as he needed them. But that wasn't true. Zacchaeus needed them *more*.

If Macoa acted on the threat of economic sanctions, it would cripple Kirtida's economy. Worse still, his people would no longer have the wheat so many depended on for their livelihood. Without Mattan and Aidara adding weight to any retaliation, Kirtida would be forced to give in to Macoa's demands.

And giving in would kill his father.

It wasn't an option.

'It might not change what I'd do,' she continued now, her voice no longer heated with the passion she'd just spoken with. 'But it would make me feel better about marrying you. So, I'll ask one more time. Will you spend time with me?'

'I'm a king. I don't have time—'

'*Make* time,' she insisted. 'Make time to get to know the woman who's going to be beside you while you rule your kingdom.'

He so badly wanted to say yes. Not only because something about her made him want to give her exactly what she asked for, but also because saying yes would mean that he wouldn't have the much harder task of avoiding her. Of pretending that he didn't have secrets to keep from her. Like his father's illness, his mother's fleeing—and the mess his mother's actions had left for him to clean up.

But he couldn't say yes. Not when spending time with her would put all those secrets at risk. He ignored the reasons he felt that way—ignored the beseeching expression on Nalini's face that had just as much of an effect on his chest as her beauty did. No, he thought. He couldn't spend time with her.

'I'm sorry, Nalini. I can't agree to that.'

'You can't agree to spend time with me?'

Nalini's heart thumped in her chest as she said the words, a sick feeling settling in her stomach. She'd thought that when Zacchaeus had told her he knew she was on Kirtida to get to know him as well as to plan the wedding, it had meant that he'd been willing to play along.

Asking him to spend time with her had felt too much like begging, and now his refusal of her... It felt intensely personal. As if he *could* make time but wouldn't because he didn't *want* to spend it with her.

'And you really think I'm going to spend all my time planning a wedding?'

'I'll have my secretary draw up a list of things you can do on Kirtida. You'll be so busy you won't even notice that you're alone.'

She gave a short bark of laughter. 'Has that ever worked for you?'

His eyes narrowed. 'I'm not sure what you mean.'

'You're alone here, aren't you? Your parents don't live in the castle and whatever relationship you had with them must have been spoilt the moment you became King. I can't imagine you have any friends, and you're holding your allies hostage. So tell me, Zacchaeus, whether you've ever been so *busy* that you haven't noticed you're alone?'

The expression on his face twisted with an emotion she couldn't identify, and then went blank so quickly she doubted her eyes. But when he spoke the coldness in his voice told her she hadn't imagined it.

'If I agree to spend time with you, Nalini… What happens then?' His brows lifted. 'You've already told me you'll marry me, and you're implying that you trust me to act as we agreed by doing that. So what happens if you get to know me and it *doesn't* make you feel better?'

'It…it would—'

'It might not,' he interrupted mildly. 'You already have all the proof you need to show you that I'm not a good man. I've overthrown my father to become King, so you know I'm power-hungry. My parents don't live in the castle any more, so you know I'm cruel.' He pushed away his plate and leaned his forearms on the table, angling himself so that she had no choice but to look into the arresting lines of his face. 'I demanded that you marry me without even asking you how you felt about it, so you know I only care about what I want. Do you really want to get to know a man like that?'

'You *want* me to see that man,' she said, fighting to keep the panic she felt from her voice. 'For some reason, *you* think it's easier.'

'No, Nalini. *You're* the one who thinks this situation is easier than it is.' He sat back now. 'You're hoping that I'm not that man, and that's why you want to get to know me. But I'm sorry, I don't have time to quell your fears. You told me *you* made this choice. And the thing about making choices is that you have to deal with their consequences.'

She suddenly wanted to scream at him, to tell him that she *knew* everything about choices and their consequences. She could still feel the girls pulling at her jewellery and clothes that night on the beach. She could still hear the boys laughing at her panic. Worst of all, she could still see

Josh's face as he laughed with them, the person who'd told her he'd keep her safe gone, leaving only the sick realisation that he'd never existed.

And then there was the way her family had reacted after...

The fact that she was on Kirtida, having this conversation with him, *was* her dealing with the consequences of her actions.

But, of course, she could voice none of that.

'Fine,' she said quietly. 'I won't waste my time trying to find some redeeming quality in you.'

She saw the surprise but it faded quickly. 'Good. Because you won't.' With those words, he walked out of the room.

She sat there for a moment, not entirely sure what to do, and then stood. It took her another few minutes to figure out that she didn't know where her room was, and was about to ask when a young woman came up to her.

'Your Royal Highness, His Majesty King Zacchaeus has asked me to show you to your room.'

Nalini's chest loosened in relief. 'Thank you.'

She followed the woman—Sylvia—as her thoughts swirled around what had just happened. She had been so sure that Zacchaeus had wanted to say yes to her. That he would have said yes to her, but that he'd stopped himself.

Or had that just been in her mind?

She hated the uncertainty, that special kind of doubt that she hadn't felt in nine years. Or perhaps the kind of doubt she'd felt every day for those nine years. But it felt more acute now, though that was probably normal. Nalini hadn't made a decision of her own—not really—in that amount of time. She shouldn't be surprised now, after she had, that she was being reminded of the fears that had stemmed from that fateful night.

She reminded herself that this decision had been nothing like the one nine years ago. Nalini had gone into *this* one with her eyes open. And yes, perhaps she'd hoped that Zacchaeus would be on the same page as her. That she could find some common ground between them so that marrying him wouldn't be so completely terrifying. But now that she knew where she stood, she had to accept it.

She *would* accept it.

She murmured her thanks to Sylvia when they got to the room, and waited to be alone before she looked around. Like the rest of the castle, the room was a mixture of old and new. It was spacious, the walls and beige carpet no doubt old, but modernised by a king-size bed covered in white that matched the chiffon curtains. Large windows stood above a chaise longue and Nalini immediately opened them, breathing in the fresh sea air.

The day had changed, she noted. The sun had been eclipsed by clouds, the sky a grey colour that felt ominous. The water thrashed against the pier that was visible from her window, and when she leaned forward she could see the faint outline of the castle of Mattan.

The longing for home pulsed in her veins but she knew she couldn't go back. Perhaps that was why the longing felt so desperate. If she went back she would be returning to a life she'd never thought she'd have. A life where she did everything that was expected of her just so that she could prove she'd learnt from her mistakes.

But she'd seen how her sister, Alika, and Xavier's lives had turned out because they'd followed all the expectations of them. It had made them incredibly unhappy, and she'd dreaded that future for herself. But she'd been afraid to do anything about it. Because once, a long time ago, she *had* done something about it and it had broken her heart—and her dreams—in one night.

But when Xavier had announced his engagement with Leyna she'd been given a glimpse of a life she could have. And when she'd last spoken with Alika she had realised her two options.

On the one hand, she could choose to disobey her mother and grandmother to protect her kingdom. They might not be happy with her decision, but for the sake of Mattan they would accept it and acknowledge that it was a responsible choice.

At least that was what she hoped.

It was an added benefit that being on Kirtida would give her the freedom of making her own decisions. She could regain that excitement for life she'd lost so long ago. She could have her independence.

On the other hand, she could listen to them and stay. She could keep on living the life she'd been living. She'd marry a man her mother and grandmother had chosen, just like Alika had, and be unhappy. Just like Alika was.

Alika would never say it aloud, but Nalini knew

her older sister. And though Nalini no longer expected love or happiness, she'd hoped for contentment at the very least. Alika had always accepted her fate without complaining. And sometimes Nalini wished she could be like that too. But she wasn't. She knew that if she wanted her chance at contentment she couldn't just accept, or do, what was expected. And Zacchaeus's proposal—*if* it could be called that—had come at exactly the right time for her to act on her realisation.

So she'd gone for the first option. Which had brought her here. To an island where she knew no one except the man who had demanded that she marry him. Who was refusing to spend any time with her, leaving her completely alone.

But she couldn't go back home.

A knock on the door roused her from her thoughts and she opened it to see Sylvia again.

'Your Royal Highness, I'm sorry to interrupt. His Majesty King Zacchaeus has requested to see you in an hour.'

Nalini frowned. 'Why?'

'I'm not sure, ma'am. All he said was that he had a proposition for you. Shall I tell him you'll be there?'

A proposition, she mused. From the man who'd turned down her own barely an hour ago.

Interesting.

'Please do.'

CHAPTER THREE

'YOU WANTED TO see me?'

Nalini's voice pulled him from his work and Zacchaeus looked up to see her standing in the doorway of his library. She had changed from earlier and was now wearing black trousers and a white shirt. The shirt was loose, cut into a V at her neck, and gave him only the barest glimpse of bronze skin. It was in no way inappropriate and yet, by the way his body reacted, he could have sworn that she was hardly wearing anything.

'Yes. Did you settle in well?' he asked in a gruff voice.

'Fine, thank you,' she answered, her tone perfectly polite—cool, even—and so very different to the passionate tone she'd used earlier.

That was his fault, and he was helpless to change it. He'd acted exactly like the man he was trying to convince her he was. Power-hungry, cruel, selfish. And though he might not entirely be *that* man, he wasn't who she wanted him to be either. In fact, he was probably closer to the man he'd told her he was than the man she wanted him to be.

Or did he just believe that because of how his parents had treated him?

'Can I get you something to drink?' he asked to distract himself.

'No, thank you.' She paused. 'Why am I here?'

Right to the point then. Not that he could blame her. He gestured for her to sit and, after hesitating, she took the seat opposite him.

'I was hoping I could talk to you about something my advisors brought to my attention.'

'I'm listening.'

'Well, they seem to think your suggestion that we spend time together… They think it's a good idea.'

Her eyebrows rose. 'Really?'

'Yes.'

'But…'

'Publicly.'

'Why?'

'So that your soon-to-be people will get to

know their future Queen, as you said.' He swallowed, and wondered why he suddenly felt nervous. 'They'll get to see us together. The couple who will rule them. And it'll help them become more comfortable with the idea.'

'You had to have your advisors tell you that it would be a good idea?'

'They had a good point.'

'You just didn't want to hear that point from me?'

He kept his mouth shut. Because he couldn't tell her the truth. That he *had* thought she'd made a good point, but was worried that it wouldn't turn out as positive as she'd made it seem. His kingdom had been...*tense* since Zacchaeus had become King and though they had seemed relieved that he was marrying Nalini, preserving the alliance between the isles, he didn't want to tempt fate. Not until he had the chance to speak to his advisors.

'So what would this entail?'

'It would be a business agreement,' he answered. 'We'd make appointments to arrange things for the wedding. Together. Publicly.'

The time she took to respond had him holding his breath.

'I had a conversation with Sylvia when you sent her to ask me here this evening. The woman who showed me to my room?'

'Yes, I know.'

'Just making sure,' she said easily. Her expression gave nothing away. Unless, of course, it did, and he just couldn't read it because he didn't know her. 'She was telling me how... *challenging* it's been for the kingdom to accept their new King.'

He clenched his teeth. So much for not telling her about that. 'You must have misheard.'

'No, I don't think I did.' Her eyes darkened. 'Clearly your advisors are trying to help you regain the trust of your people after the coup. And how better than a wedding? To remind them of the traditions of the royal family. Make them believe in fairy tales. Weddings are the start of something beautiful, hopeful, and seeing the King who ended the reign of their well-loved ruler—his father—at a new beginning might just make them more open to *his* new beginning. As King.'

'You're right. But I needed to check with them to make sure that what you were suggesting would work.'

He saw the surprise, but she only nodded. 'That's fair, I suppose.'

'So you agree?'

'I don't exactly have a choice, do I?' She clasped her hands together on her lap and he found himself saying words he knew he shouldn't be saying.

'You have a choice, Nalini. You'll always have a choice here.'

Emotion filled her eyes before it was replaced by cool indifference. 'Of course I will. I only meant that it wasn't like I could return to Mattan.' She blinked and quickly added, 'Because it would put them in danger.'

'That's not what you meant.'

'What else could I possibly mean?'

'That's what I'm asking.' He studied her, noting that she was avoiding looking at him and knew his gut feeling had been right. 'There's more to why you're here, Nalini, isn't there?'

'You didn't exactly propose this arrangement as a question.'

'Yes, but you've already told me *you* chose to do this. Tell me why.'

'I have,' she replied stubbornly. 'I'm here for Mattan.'

'And yet the more I get to know you, the more I think that isn't the only reason.'

'But since this is a business arrangement, as *you* said, I don't have to tell you anything other than what I want to.'

Her face lit with the challenge, but there was a dullness in her eyes that...that *bothered* him. He couldn't place a finger on why—wasn't sure he wanted to—and instead he asked, 'So, you agree then?'

'Yes.'

'Great. We'll make appointments to plan the wedding. I'll have my secretary arrange a schedule for us and I'll send it to you for approval.'

She nodded. 'Is that all?'

'No, actually there's one more thing.' But he couldn't bring himself to say the words.

'You have something planned already, don't you?' Her mouth relaxed into what he thought was the beginning of a smile. His body tightened.

'*I* don't have anything planned. But there is…a plan. An appointment for us, really.'

'What is it?'

'An…engagement shoot. Tomorrow.' Damn it, he felt foolish even *saying* it.

'An engagement shoot,' she repeated, and laughed. It was a soft, happy sound that made him think of a music box. 'You must hate the thought of that so much.'

'It has to be done.'

'Of course,' she responded in a grave tone that echoed his, but her eyes sparkled with laughter.

His lips twitched. 'So, you're fine with this?'

'My schedule happens to be open,' she said wryly. 'Why not?'

'Good.' He frowned. 'I didn't expect it to be that easy.'

'I'm here to serve at your pleasure, Your Majesty.'

It took some time for her to realise that she'd said something provocative, and when she did her eyes widened and colour flooded her skin.

'I didn't mean—'

He couldn't help the smile now, even though his attempts at dimming his body's reaction to her unintended suggestion had proved futile. 'I know.'

'It's because you make me nervous.'

'Why?'

'I'm not entirely sure.' She gave him a chagrined smile, but there was emotion on her face that paralysed him and he couldn't look away. 'Maybe it's because today was the first time you and I have really spoken. The events we've seen each other at...' Her voice faded and he quickly figured out why.

He'd kept himself apart from the Mattanian and Aidaraen royal families at those events. Oh, he'd greeted, had done his duty, but the ease that had always been between the two families hadn't included him. Of his own accord, he knew, and realised that Nalini was referring to that one-sidedness he'd embraced. But he'd known what was at risk if he'd become one of them. His family's most well-kept secret.

His mother's affair.

'Or it could just be because you're a little scary, King Zacchaeus.'

Despite what he'd been thinking of, that drew a smile from him. 'You're not the first person to say that.'

'No, I don't imagine I am,' she replied softly, and her mouth curved up in the smallest of smiles.

For the first time, Zacchaeus realised he was in trouble. No, he corrected, taking in what that smile did to the already lovely features of her face—*and* what it did to his heart rate. He'd known he was in trouble the moment he'd come up with the hare-brained plan to marry Nalini.

He'd convinced himself, just as he had Xavier, Leyna and Nalini, that it had been for the sake of the alliance. And, up until that moment, he'd believed that that was the only reason. Except now he remembered how often his eyes had strayed to Nalini at every event. How her smile, polite as it had been, had made it the tiniest bit harder to breathe.

He thought about how he'd felt after he'd left the discussion with Leyna and Xavier the day he'd told them of his plan—the anger at their responses, the fear that it would put Kirtida at risk—and how it had changed when he'd seen Nalini in the castle passage. He'd felt longing. Hope.

And he'd wished with all his might that his hare-brained plan would work just so that he could have that feeling for the rest of his life.

'Does it bother you?' she asked, studying him. For one irrational moment he thought she was asking about his feelings for her. 'That people think you're scary, I mean,' she clarified, and he told himself to get a grip.

'I don't care what people think of me,' he said in a cool tone, hoping it would have the same effect on his emotions. 'What I care about is that they do what they're supposed to do. What I ask them to.'

'I'm afraid you might not entirely succeed in that with me.'

'Yes,' he answered wryly. 'I didn't think I would.'

'Now *you're* not the first person to say that about me.'

He rested his forearms on his thighs and leaned

forward. 'Do you mean Princess Nalini of Mattan was a problem child?'

'Depends on who you ask,' she said lightly, but all trace of humour disappeared from her face. 'What should I wear for the shoot?'

The change in subject happened so quickly, so smoothly, that he had to take a moment to adjust. And, though he didn't press, it intrigued him.

'I've arranged for a few dresses to be sent to your room. You can choose whichever one you'd feel most comfortable in.'

She nodded. 'Are we done?'

'For now.'

'Then I'll see you tomorrow.' She stood and smoothed the fabric of her trousers.

'I'll see you tomorrow,' he repeated and got up with her. They stood like that as the seconds passed and then she finally walked to the door, but turned back before going through it.

'One meal.' When he lifted his eyebrows, she continued. 'We'll share one meal a day. You can choose whichever one you'd like.'

He wanted to smile at the brazen request—at the *nerve*—but all he gave her was a grudging, 'Fine.' She walked out then, and Zacchaeus's eyes stayed on the door until he realised he had no reason to keep staring at it.

He walked to his desk and, leaning back in his chair, took in the view through the glass doors leading to his balcony. The night was clear, seemingly unaffected by the misery of the afternoon. And, as he had so many times before, he silently thanked the designer who'd made sure the furniture arrangement would give him an unobstructed view of the sea.

The stretch of water always gave him a sense of purpose and, right now, he had to accept that that purpose was to protect his kingdom. And protecting his kingdom meant focusing on the negotiations he was having with Leyna and Xavier and getting to his wedding day so that he would finally be able to sign the papers that would ensure it.

He couldn't afford to be enthralled by his fiancée. He couldn't even afford to *like* her—*if* he listened to his father. Jaydon had warned him against trusting Nalini, though Zacchaeus knew Jaydon's warning had come from his own experience with Zacchaeus's mother.

The woman who'd caused the drama he was currently dealing with.

Zacchaeus couldn't even be glad that she wasn't in Kirtida any more. Not when her departure had made his father's already weak heart worsen. Not when her leaving was the reason that Zacchaeus had been forced into being King before he'd been ready. Not when she was the reason his kingdom was being threatened by sanctions—perhaps even by war—because Kirtida couldn't give in to Macoa's demands.

Not if Zacchaeus wanted to keep his father alive.

Perhaps not liking Nalini *was* the best route to go. If only he could figure out how…

CHAPTER FOUR

'THIS IS ABSOLUTELY RIDICULOUS,' Zacchaeus grumbled under his breath, and Nalini grinned. It was impossible not to smile at his grumpiness, especially when she was quite enjoying herself.

'Oh, stop frowning,' she said. 'Or people will think that you don't really want to marry me.'

'Or they'll think I really hate pictures. Especially fluffy ones.'

'Fluffy pictures?' she repeated. 'Are there cute, fluffy animals around that I haven't seen yet?'

'You know what I mean.'

'Zacchaeus,' she said, and took his hand as they walked down to the castle's gardens where they would be taking the so-called fluffy pictures.

As soon as she realised what she'd done, she snatched her hand back—how had that felt so *natural*?—and gestured for the photographer to continue. She waited until the two of them were alone. 'I know you don't like this, but we have to make it believable.'

'I thought I was doing a pretty good job.'

'You were. But the pictures we just took were official ones, in the confines of the castle. Now we're out here—' she lifted her arms '—in the gorgeous garden of the castle, with the gorgeous trees and colours around us. You have to make more of an effort.'

He narrowed his eyes. 'Are you always this… optimistic?'

Her lips twitched at the disgust in his tone. 'The quickest answer to that is yes.'

'Even though they're taking fake photographs to celebrate our fake engagement?'

'It may not be the traditional way people choose to marry, but it isn't fake.' Nalini fought to keep her voice light, though he was dampening her enjoyment. 'In fact, this is probably as real as it's ever going to be for us.'

'*That* doesn't sound optimistic.'

'Sometimes realism slips in before I get to shine it with positivity.' But she sighed, and felt her mood turn to match his. 'Look, the simplest way for us to get through this is to make it look genuine. No one would question our commitment if they look at the pictures and any onlookers will feel as though they've seen something worth looking at.'

She paused when they reached the path, and decided to tell him what she really thought. 'That means you probably shouldn't touch me like I'm some wounded animal you'd like to save but are disgusted by because you found it on the street.'

His lips curved. 'That's quite the vivid image.'

'Yes, well.' She sniffed. 'I've always had a talent with words.'

'So I'm beginning to see.' He stared at her for a beat longer than she was comfortable with, and then nodded. 'Fine. I'll stop complaining.' He pulled at the neck of the uniform he looked so dashing in with the words, 'And I'll pretend to be in love with you. Or, at the bare minimum, in lust.'

'You just have to look as though you're interested in me,' she said quickly, not wanting to dwell on the way her heart skipped at the thought of either of those options. 'So stop frowning, for heaven's sake, and focus on the fact that it *is* a beautiful day. And that your kingdom will probably respond positively to your efforts.'

She hurried after the photographer then, afraid his teasing would turn into something else. She wasn't worried that that something else would be physical. She had no interest in exploring that, no matter how attractive she found him. Or how he felt about her, she thought, remembering the heat in his eyes when he'd seen her in the blush knee-length dress she'd chosen for the engagement photos.

No, she was more worried about how he got her to reveal things about herself that she didn't want anyone to know. Like the fact that she'd never told anyone that she felt like a problem child. Not even Xavier or Alika. Though she was sure that if she told them they wouldn't be surprised.

They all knew about *that day*—as her mother liked to call it—which had really been the only time in Nalini's life that she'd outright disobeyed her parents. But the consequences had been so far-reaching that it had tainted the years since. For her family *and* herself.

It was the reason she was on Kirtida, marrying a man she didn't know for the sake of her kingdom. It was the reason she was trying so damn hard to make things work between them. She wanted to prove to herself—to her family—that it hadn't been a mistake. That her hopes of changing their perspective of her, of her actions, would pan out. That she wasn't just giving them another reason to think that she was reckless.

Not for the first time, Nalini thought of how much easier her life would have been if she'd been more like Alika. Willing to accept and obey. But she also knew that *easy* meant different things to different people. Yes, it meant less conflict and more safety. She knew because she *had* been more like Alika since *that day*. But it had also kept her living in a little box, so confined, so *afraid* that she'd felt as if the real her—the excited, happy her—had been whittled away slowly until she was only that way with her siblings.

And not because she wanted to be. Because she thought *they* needed it.

Even though it hadn't been there before that afternoon, Nalini twisted the engagement ring on her finger as though the nervous habit had accompanied her all her life. She'd been surprised when Zacchaeus had offered it to her, but he'd done it so unceremoniously that she hadn't had the chance to feel emotional about it.

Not that she *would* have felt emotional, she told herself. She didn't expect love or romance any more—wishing for such things was foolish. She'd learnt her lesson with Josh, hadn't she? Besides, she only had to look at her siblings to confirm it. Sure, Xavier's life was a lot happier now that he'd found love with his one-time best friend, but he'd gone through plenty of heartache before he'd got there.

No, Nalini wasn't interested in love or romance any more. What she *was* interested in was making sure her family knew that she'd changed. She also wanted autonomy in her life, and love wasn't going to give her that. An arranged marriage, on the other hand…

She stopped when she found the photographer, and watched as he squinted against the late afternoon sun. The man had insisted that they take the outdoor photos then, though now Nalini wasn't entirely sure he was confident in that decision. He cursed as he worked, taking practice shots of the stream that led down to a large pond.

'Is it just me, or does it feel like we're interrupting something?' Zacchaeus's voice sounded in her ear just as it had the day before, on the boat. Now, though, Nalini didn't have the sea breeze to blame for the shiver that went up her spine.

But you're not interested in acting on it, a voice in her head told her in a mocking tone that she didn't appreciate.

'Artists,' she replied. 'Temperamental creatures.'

'That's a broad statement.'

'And not one I thought you'd call me on,' she said with a smile. 'I don't think all artists are temperamental. I do think this one is, which is why we'd better get into that frame before it's night and we have to do this again tomorrow.'

'You're right,' Zacchaeus said and took her hand, dragging her to the stream. 'Are we okay here, Stefan?'

'Yes, sir, that's perfect,' Stefan answered, but took at least a dozen more shots before getting to them. 'Could you please move closer together?'

'I told you,' Nalini murmured and took a step forward to close the distance between her and Zacchaeus. Her heart immediately thumped louder, harder, in her chest and she stopped before she touched him.

'Why does it feel like you're the one treating *me* like a disgusting wounded animal now?' he asked, and placed a hand at the bottom of her spine. With little effort he pressed her against him, and her heart rocketed—out of her chest and, she was pretty sure, out of her body.

It hadn't been like this before. Their official photos had been close, yes, but there she'd been at his side. There she'd held his hand, which wasn't as bad as she'd thought it would be. But being face to face like this, their bodies aligned...

It made that attraction a lot harder to ignore. Especially since her mind chose to pay attention to the hard muscles of his body right at that moment.

'Your Royal Highness, could you move closer?' Stefan called from behind his camera.

'Yes, Your Royal Highness,' Zacchaeus teased. 'Move closer.'

'I think I'm close enough,' she answered, but pressed her body a fraction closer to his.

'Now smile,' Stefan called again, and now *Nalini* felt as though the entire thing was ridiculous.

But she had to acknowledge that it was only ridiculous because she had to focus on making sure Zacchaeus didn't think he was making her nervous while remembering to smile *and* to relax her body.

'Turn your heads to face one another,' Stefan asked after a few minutes, and Nalini held her breath as she turned back to face Zacchaeus. Without prompting, Zacchaeus slid his arms around her waist. Her breath caught, and Nalini wondered—illogically, she knew—what it would feel like if the action hadn't been forced for the sake of the photos.

If it had been more…intimate.

The thought sent a wave of heat to her face and she ducked her head, hoping that Zacchaeus wouldn't notice it. He banished that hope by moving his mouth to her ear and whispering, 'What's wrong?'

'Nothing.'

'You're lying.'

'I'm not,' she said, her voice sharper than she intended.

'Nalini.'

The tone of his voice had her looking up again.

And the moment she did she realised she'd made a mistake.

She hadn't noticed before that his eyes held specks of light around the irises. It made his face less intimidating, she thought, and wanted to reach up to smooth the creases between his eyebrows to make it even less so.

'That's *perfect*!' Stefan shouted, shocking her hands into immobility. 'Now kiss!'

Her entire body froze as Zacchaeus's eyes instantly changed from amused to something darker. To something more intense. Electricity crackled from them, hitting her with a voltage that woke all her nerves. It startled her, the intense response of her body to his.

And suddenly she became aware of how taut his muscles had become, how hers had responded. If she kissed him, if she just *touched* her lips to his, maybe that tension would ease…

Before Nalini fully knew what had happened,

pain stunned the breath from her as she found herself on her butt. The bottom half of her body was completely wet from the water of the stream she now sat in. It took a moment for her brain to realise what had happened, but she didn't fully have the time to contemplate it before she heard a splash of water.

'Nalini, are you okay?' Zacchaeus asked, crouching beside her.

'I'm fine.' She was pretty sure that she was, at least. 'You shouldn't be in here though. You'll spoil your uniform.'

'It'll survive,' he said wryly and offered her a hand. 'Will you accept my help or are you going to ignore it to avoid touching me?'

'Don't be silly,' she answered, though she hesitated before she took his hand. When she was standing, she looked down at her dress, no longer falling in an A-line around her hips but flattened to her sides. 'I've spoilt this dress.' She looked up at him. 'You shouldn't have come in and spoilt your uniform too.'

'The uniform doesn't matter, Nalini. Neither does your dress. But you do.' His eyes searched her face. 'Are you sure you're okay?'

'Of course I am,' she replied, straightening her spine. Trying to maintain what little dignity she had left. 'Besides my pride, I'm perfectly fine.'

'I have to agree on that one.'

'You do? Why?'

'My pride's tingling a bit too. After all, you *did* just fall into a stream to get away from me.'

'That's *not* what happened,' she retorted, and then frowned. Was that really the reason she'd fallen into the stream? To get away from Zacchaeus? Now that the fogginess of the stun had cleared, she could remember taking a step back, away from him—*no*, she corrected. Away from *kissing* him. She hadn't meant to make it obvious. She'd just wanted space to think, and to get away from the way her body felt when she touched him.

To get away from how her body had reacted to the prospect of *kissing* him.

Of course her attempt at subtlety had landed her on her butt in a stream.

At that moment her eyes took in their spectators, clamouring against the fence surrounding the garden, their faces a mixture of surprise and concern. The faces of those she could see, that was, considering the number of phones she saw capturing everything that was happening.

Stefan had a horrified expression on his face, although she had noted while Zacchaeus had been helping her that he'd still been taking photos. And then there was Zacchaeus's face, wrought with concern and annoyance.

All of it should have embarrassed Nalini. And, she supposed, she would feel that way later, when she'd had time to process it all. But right then the only logical response she could manage started low in her belly, bubbling up her throat until she couldn't control the giggles any more.

'How are you laughing at this?' Zacchaeus asked, his eyes wide.

'Because...' She told herself to stop laughing, to answer him, but the more she tried, the more she kept laughing. 'It's just...so...*ridiculous*!' she managed between fits of laughter. 'I'm sorry, Zacchaeus,' she said, wiping a tear from her eyes. 'I know this must seem like a terribly inappropriate response, but I landed on my butt trying to get away—'

She broke off at the deep sound that came from the man in front of her. He was *laughing*. Time ticked by, and still he laughed. The shock of seeing Zacchaeus laugh lasted only a few more seconds before she found herself joining him. She wasn't sure how long they laughed together—she didn't even care that there were witnesses to their momentary insanity. And when the laughter faded there was a sparkle in his eyes that had never been there before.

It made those light flecks in his eyes that she'd only just noticed even more visible. Again, she wondered how she'd missed it, and felt unsettled, like a speck of dust that had been blown away.

'It's no wonder you don't laugh very often,' she murmured softly. 'You'd have the entire female population falling at your feet.'

CHAPTER FIVE

ZACCHAEUS TILTED HIS HEAD, acknowledging—but refusing to dwell on—the warmth that went through his body at her words. 'Is that so?'

Though her cheeks pinked, she nodded. 'I think so.'

'Because my laughter is so charming?'

'Because it makes you look...like a man,' she said. 'Not like a king.'

Caught by the picture she was painting, even though he *knew* it would only start trouble, he asked, 'Does no one notice the man when he's a king?'

'No,' she said softly, her eyes following the hand he didn't seem able to control as it swept a piece of her hair from her face. 'People look at the deeds of a king. That's how they notice his heart.'

'Which means people think I have no heart,' he said before he could stop himself.

He paused and gave himself a moment to stuff the emotions he was feeling back into the box he'd created in his mind especially for them. It was harder than it generally was, and he ignored the inner voice telling him it was because of the woman in front of him.

No, he told himself. His feelings were just becoming harder to cope with because there had been so many of them over the last months. Feelings about his mother's affair, about her leaving. About the demands she and her lover in Macoa were making of Kirtida. About his father's illness, and the fact that he'd forced Zacchaeus to pretend to overthrow him…

There had been no time to deal with them—no time to even *think* of them. But a part of him warned that he would have to face them at some stage. And that if that time didn't come soon, they might just bubble over, forcing him to deal with them.

Though it left a sick feeling in his stomach, it helped him remember he couldn't think of himself as a man—however tempting it was, he thought, looking at the woman who drew him in unlike any other. He *was* a king. Which was why he had to ignore the betrayal, the sadness, the hurt swirling around inside him because of his parents.

Which was why he had to refuse the attraction he felt towards the woman in front of him. He *had* to focus on his kingdom. He had no other choice because *he was King*.

And a king shouldn't be standing in a stream with his fiancée, laughing at something that could be misconstrued.

'We should probably get out of here,' he said, keeping his voice devoid of emotion. And keeping his heart devoid of it too, when it wanted to react to the way her face fell.

'You're right,' she said after a few moments and aimed unsettlingly cool eyes at Stefan. 'Can you make do with what you have, Stefan? I'd prefer not to repeat this process.'

It was a jab at him, he thought. And it hit its mark.

'Yes, ma'am.' Stefan rushed forward now and helped Nalini out of the stream. 'I will edit these pictures immediately and have them sent to the castle for approval.'

'Thank you,' Nalini answered as she stepped

onto the grass. Water ran down her legs—long and shapely in the heels she wore—and Zacchaeus had to force his eyes away from them to look for someone who could assist them.

He strode to the nearest staff member he saw and requested that towels be brought to them as soon as possible. When he returned to Nalini and Stefan, Nalini was thanking the photographer again in a voice significantly warmer than the one he'd heard her use before he'd left.

'I'm sure the pictures will come out beautifully,' she said before turning to him. Her eyes went cool again, and something chilled inside him as well.

He told himself that it had nothing to do with the fact that she was filled with light and happiness. That her laughing at something that she could have found embarrassing had been so authentic that he thought it was the first time he'd seen a glimpse of the real Nalini.

Which had him wondering why she thought that she needed to hide the real her.

He shook his head, grateful for the distraction of being brought the towels he'd asked for. He took them and handed one to Nalini.

'You should dry off.'

'I'd prefer to have a shower,' she answered, but took the towel and rubbed it over her legs. She slipped out of her heels and dried her feet and, though he was tempted to keep watching her—what *was* it about her legs that was so captivating?—it reminded him that his feet were wet too.

Like her, he wanted a shower. *And* dry clothes and shoes. Since he'd angled his body so that she would have some privacy from the onlookers, he couldn't dry himself off as she was doing. Yet he was hesitant to leave.

That burst of light he'd seen from her had been so refreshing—and so completely different from the perpetual darkness he'd felt shroud him since the night of the State Banquet. Since before then, he knew, thinking about his mother.

He didn't want to return to that darkness—not yet, anyway. The only way he could see that not happening was if he continued to spend time with her. Because even though he'd managed to dim the light somewhat, he didn't think she'd let it be dimmed for long.

'We'll have dinner in half an hour,' he told her.

'Fine.'

'You're okay with that?'

'Of course I am. I was the one who asked that we share a meal. Dinner is the only meal left today.' She handed the towel back to the woman who'd brought it and picked up her shoes, dangling them from two fingers. 'I hope you feel better once you get out of those clothes.'

'I feel fine.'

She smiled now, an almost feline look that sent a stab of desire through him. 'I was trying to be nice. I meant that I hope your attitude changes. Away from the King and into the man. I like him.'

She didn't wait for a reply and left him speechless. But he was beginning to realise that that was just the effect she had on him. He released a breath, and then forced his feet to make their way back to his room. Stefan immediately fell into step beside him, offering an apology for the way things had turned out, which Zacchaeus waved away.

But he supposed he couldn't blame the people who worked for him for walking on eggshells. Before his father had stepped down, things hadn't been going particularly well in the castle. Jaydon had lived with his heart disease for years, but it had taken its toll on him. Especially in recent years. He had been determined to keep his illness to himself, only telling Zacchaeus because he'd wanted 'the future King of Kirtida to be prepared'. And when the whispers about him being ill had started, Jaydon had tightened the reins of his rule with those around him, hoping to dispel any rumours of weakness.

But his illness, combined with the weight of the secret he'd been keeping and the fact that things had been getting worse with Zacchaeus's mother, had made Jaydon miserable. His misery had made him unbearable. And since no one— including Zacchaeus's mother—knew why, his mood seemed uncalled for, and so unlike the King many of the staff loved and respected.

It had got worse when Zacchaeus's mother had left. Michelle had claimed that Jaydon's moods weren't what she'd signed on for but, considering the rocky state of their marriage for the last thirty years, Zacchaeus had known she'd merely been looking for an excuse to leave.

That, and the fact that she'd left in the middle of the night with only a brief note explaining her absence.

Now that his kingdom was being threatened, Zacchaeus knew exactly why she'd left. Michelle had known that she would never have got away if they'd got wind of her plans. But after she'd left, and they'd heard she'd arrived in Macoa, his father had taken a turn for the worse.

Zacchaeus had barely had the chance to process it all before his father had asked him to stage the coup. Jaydon hadn't wanted anyone—especially his estranged wife and her lover—to know he was stepping down because he was ill. Two months later, Zacchaeus was still too consumed—now with trying to protect Kirtida—to think about it and the complications his father had created by asking him to do something he really hadn't wanted to.

He shook off the thoughts and nearly rolled his eyes when his staff hurriedly cleared the way for him when he entered the castle. They were so afraid of him, he thought with a frown. Not only because of the nervousness his father had instilled in them, but because they saw Zacchaeus as the man who'd overthrown his own father because of his desire for power. It didn't seem to matter that many of them had witnessed him growing up and knew that he hadn't always been the man they saw him as now.

So he brushed it all off and pretended that none of it bothered him. But he knew it did, and it was only having Nalini there to remind him of more than just the darkness that gave him some reprieve.

He thought of how he'd felt when he'd seen her in that beautiful pale pink dress. When he'd seen the way her skin had looked almost gold against it. When he'd noticed her shapely legs, and had longed to touch the curls that framed her face.

He hadn't anticipated the way his heart would race when he was close to her. Or the way his body would tighten. He hadn't expected honesty from her, even when it was clear that it embarrassed her. It was almost as though she couldn't help herself.

And it was all so refreshing that Zacchaeus constantly wanted to be around her—despite his warnings to himself.

But since he knew he couldn't afford to dwell on it all, he got ready quickly, forcing himself to ignore how he felt when he saw Nalini already waiting for him when he was done. She stood when he entered the dining hall, and the air in his lungs thickened when he saw that she'd changed into another dress.

This one was floral, flared slightly at the hips, just like the dress she'd worn for the photo shoot. It suited her body, he thought. And then told himself that thinking about her body would only get him into trouble when it became even harder to breathe.

'Am I late?'

'I only got here a few minutes ago, so you're okay.' After he'd helped her into her seat, he took his own. 'Feeling better now?' she asked once he had.

He couldn't help the smile that crept onto his lips. 'I think so.'

'Wonderful,' she said easily, giving him a slight nod. 'It might have been awkward otherwise.'

He laughed softly. 'Do you always say what you're thinking?'

'No,' she replied indignantly. 'I'm a princess. I *have* to think before I speak.'

'So everything you say to me is well thought-out?'

'No,' she said again. 'For some reason it doesn't seem to work with you.' There was a pause, and then she laughed a little breathlessly. 'See?'

He stared at her, and then slowly shook his head. 'I can't quite figure you out, Nalini.'

'It doesn't seem like you *have* to figure me out.' She lifted her shoulders. 'I'm more honest with you than I'd like to be, after all.'

'Oh, I don't think *that's* true.'

'But I'm agreeing with what you just said.'

'I know, and I believe that you can't help but be honest with me. *Sometimes*,' he said, and told himself to tread carefully. 'You shut me out yesterday when I asked if you were a problem child.'

He could almost feel her recoil, just as she had the day before. 'No, I answered you.'

'But you pulled away. Just like you're doing now.'

She tilted her head. 'Isn't this strange?'

The tone of her voice put his back up. 'What?'

'This.' She waved between them. 'The fact that you think *I'm* pulling away from you when you didn't even want to give me a chance to get to know *you* at first.'

'I told you why.'

'No, you told me why you didn't want to plan our wedding together. But even now that we are planning it together, or will be, you've called it a *business arrangement*. Which, by definition, means you don't want to talk about anything personal.'

'That's not…' He trailed off, struggling to find the words to explain himself. 'It's not the same thing.'

'Of course you won't see it that way.' She fell silent when the starters arrived and the wine was poured, and only continued when they were alone again. 'Would you like to prove me wrong? Tell me something about yourself.'

'I already have, Nalini,' he said, annoyance masking the faint panic.

'Like what?' She picked up her knife and fork, and then lifted her brows when he didn't answer. 'See? You haven't shared anything personal with me.'

'Oh, I have,' he answered, picking up his utensils too. 'I remember because it was something

I shouldn't have told you.' He froze as soon as he realised what he'd said, wondering how he'd fallen into the trap of saying too much. Again.

Silence followed his words, and Zacchaeus felt the tension slowly make its way up his back and across his shoulders. And then she asked, 'What's your favourite colour?'

'What?'

'Your favourite colour,' she repeated. 'I'm giving you an easy out here. Take it.'

It took a few seconds for him to process and then he said, 'Green.'

'Favourite book?'

'I don't have one.' He shrugged. 'I prefer movies.'

'I'm not sure I can give you an out on that one.' She shook her head. 'In fact, I don't think I've ever been more disappointed in you.'

He laughed, and wondered how she'd managed to defuse the tension. 'I'm sure that's not true.'

'It is if we start counting from the start of this dinner. Which I am.'

'Okay.' The smile he gave her came more naturally now. 'What's your favourite colour?'

'Pink.' She widened her eyes. 'A massive surprise, I know. A princess liking pink.'

'It suits you.'

The surprise on her face was genuine now. 'How would you know?'

'Your dress today. You looked…nice in it.' Which was the understatement of the year, he thought.

'That was blush.'

'It was pink.'

'Ah, yes, the male colour spectrum,' she answered and sipped her wine. 'Where all colours that kind of look the same *are* the same.'

'Exactly.' He grinned. 'What was your favourite thing to do on Mattan?'

Her smile wavered and he cursed himself for bringing up the home he was responsible for taking her away from. He tried to think of another question—one that would bring back the ease that had somehow settled between them—but she answered him before he could.

'Painting.' Her voice was soft. 'I love putting colour on a canvas. Making something that started out as nothing into something.'

'You paint?'

'Not very well, but yes, I do.'

'I don't believe you.'

'Well, you'll have to,' she answered. 'You have no proof that I paint well.'

'I will,' he vowed. 'Soon too.'

'Really? How do you intend to find out? It's not like you can call anyone on Mattan to ask.' Her eyes widened immediately. 'Oh, I'm so sorry, Zacchaeus.'

CHAPTER SIX

'FOR WHAT?' ZACCHAEUS answered easily. 'Reminding me of the reality of this relationship?'

He meant to make light of her slip-up, Nalini thought, but he hadn't *quite* got it right. Which was her own fault, she supposed, for bringing it up. But then she reminded herself that *she* hadn't really been the one to bring it up. *He'd* mentioned Mattan, and her heart had sagged with heaviness at the thought of her home.

Of the home she'd *chosen* to leave and couldn't go back to.

'I've upset you,' Nalini said softly. 'I didn't mean to.'

'You haven't upset me, Nalini.'

She studied his face and then nodded. 'So we're back to this then.'

'I'm not sure what you're talking about.'

'No?' she asked. 'You haven't just stepped

back into being King Zacchaeus, and away from getting to know me?'

'You need to stop this,' he snapped, and set down his knife and fork. 'There is no distinction between me as a man and me as a king. They're one and the same. The only reason you've claimed they aren't is because you're hoping—again—for someone who doesn't exist.'

He'd surprised her a number of times since she'd arrived at Kirtida. With his compassion, his perceptiveness. And maybe that had lured her into the fantasy that they could at least be friends. But there would be no friendship with Zacchaeus, she told herself. She needed to remember that when the compassion came out, the perceptiveness. Because she couldn't keep feeling the disappointment tinged ever so slightly with hurt when they disappeared.

'You're right,' she answered. 'It won't happen again.'

Emotion flitted across his eyes, but it was gone too quickly for her to identify what it meant. 'Good. You're finally getting the message.'

She wanted to reply, to put him in his place, but she reined it in. It was pointless, she thought, to try and make him see sense. To try and make him realise that he didn't have to be the jerk she was sitting next to. That he *could* be the man she'd thought he was.

But trying to get him to share anything with her was exhausting, and she'd only been doing it for two days. And yes, maybe that exhaustion seemed so much worse mingled with how homesick she'd suddenly become, but she didn't have to try if he didn't.

And so she wouldn't.

It meant that the rest of their meal was eaten in complete silence. It wasn't something she was used to, the silence, and it made her throat itch to say something—*anything*—to breach it. But that would have meant that she would be trying again, and she refused to.

So each time she wanted to open her mouth to say something, she'd reach for her wine instead. Before she knew it, her glass had been refilled twice and she was feeling the slightest bit tipsy. She was glad when the dessert came and, though the chocolate mousse looked delicious, she barely tasted it in her rush to leave.

'Please excuse me,' she said as soon as her

plate was empty, and ignored the frown Zac-chaeus sent her.

'No post-supper coffee?'

'So that we could spend another thirty min-utes in silence?' she scoffed. 'I don't think that's going to help me stay sober.'

She frowned. Why had she just said that?

'You're trying to stay sober?' he asked, and she thought she saw his lips spasm.

'If you must know, yes, I am.' She lifted her chin. 'I don't like tense situations, and it seems like tonight has made me drink a bit too much.'

'Are you…drunk, Princess?'

'Of course not! But,' she allowed, 'I might be closer to it than to being sober.'

'I see,' he answered measuredly. 'Would you like me to escort you to your room?'

'Definitely not.' She took a step back, barely hearing the scrape of the chair as she did. 'You're the reason I feel this way. You're not going to swoop in and play the dashing gentleman. It'll only make me imagine you're someone you're not even more. And you don't want that.'

She looked at him and he gave her a nod,

though something in his eyes made her feel that maybe he did.

'I will escort myself to my room then. Good-night.'

Nalini turned with the words and found that her chair was still behind her, so she couldn't stalk off as she'd intended to. And now she had to decide which direction to go. If she chose the left, where the rest of the dining chairs were, she wasn't entirely sure she would be able to navigate her way past them without making herself look foolish.

If she chose the right, she would have to face Zacchaeus and...well, she was afraid that she would be drawn in by that deliciously manly smell of his. She'd got a good whiff of it when they'd been posing for the photos, and she knew that it was the kind of smell that made women swoon. And since she was a woman she had swooned too, and she didn't think she'd be able to resist it again.

Especially now, since she wasn't...feeling herself.

'Do you need help?' Zacchaeus said smoothly, only the slightest lilt of amusement in his voice.

'No, I'm fine,' she answered primly, but still she stood, unable to make the decision.

'Are you sure?'

'Would you mind getting out of the way?'

'Of course,' he answered and moved so that he was no longer to her right, but rather in front of her. It didn't help her dilemma, but she knew she couldn't delay for any longer so she walked around her chair and held her breath as she walked past him.

But she misjudged and took a breath before she was far enough away from him.

The scent hit her, and desire crawled deep in her belly. She kept her back to him, ignoring the steps she heard following her. She didn't want to turn around and test the control she had over her desire for him. Not when her mind was offering her a picture of how she'd look in his arms, her mouth on his, tasting the secrets those perfect lips had to offer.

'Are you okay?'

'I'm fine,' she answered, and found that she was. That knock of lust had somehow cleared her mind and the only thing she wanted now was to get away from him. To breathe in air that didn't tempt her but gave her comfort. 'Goodnight, Zacchaeus,' she told him again, still without looking, and walked towards the door.

In a few quick steps she made it out to the hallway and traced her way back to the garden where their pictures had been taken that afternoon. She saw a movement in the shadows and turned only to confirm that her bodyguard had joined her.

She smiled at him and then took a deep breath, hoping that somehow the air would reach all the places in her body that felt suffocated. She followed the path back to the stream she'd fallen into, and took a seat on the embankment.

She almost missed the slight tipsiness she'd felt earlier. Because now, with the fresh air clearing her brain, she felt like a failure. As if she'd made a decision and she'd failed at it yet again.

It reminded her of how Xavier had reacted when she'd decided to come to Kirtida. How he'd warned her not to be careless but to take it seriously. It reminded her of how disapproving her mother had been when she'd told them she would be marrying Zacchaeus. How it had been nothing in comparison to the way her grand-mother had reacted.

Paulina had flat-out refused that Nalini agree to Zacchaeus's demands. *'His eyes are dark, Nalini,'* Paulina had said. *'You won't be able to change that darkness until you find out what caused it, and he won't let you.'*

Suddenly she realised how much of what she'd been doing on Kirtida had been devoted to prov-ing her family—her grandmother—wrong. Pau-lina's last words to her had somehow become a symbol of her disapproval, a symbol of Nalini's entire family's disapproval of her decision.

A symbol that haunted her.

Much like the 'I told you so' they had given her when she'd returned from the beach that night so long ago, shaking with fear and disappoint-ment, her teenage heart broken and her dreams shattered.

Nalini saw now that if she'd been able to con-vince Zacchaeus to tell her about that darkness it would have been a victory for her. It would have been proof that she *had* been responsible in coming to Kirtida. And proof would have given her hope. Hope that saving her kingdom would redefine her. Perhaps it would have even been an opportunity for *her* to tell her family 'I told you so'.

But she'd been wrong. And now she had to face the reality of it.

She needed to start accepting that her family would always see her as irresponsible. That they would always see her as the daughter who'd put herself and the Crown at risk. Once she'd accepted that she could face that perhaps she just wasn't cut out for the life she'd wanted. Perhaps freedom and contentment were for people other than herself. Maybe the only life she had to look forward to was the one she'd seen Alika live. The one Xavier had lived before he'd reconciled with Leyna. A life of obedience and disappointment. Of unhappiness.

She hadn't wanted to be unhappy, but she was beginning to realise that that hope was unrealistic. Unhappiness seemed to be the fate of a royal life. Unless there'd been luck involved—as it had been with Xavier and Leyna—she couldn't think of one other royal who'd found contentment in their relationship.

Her parents and grandparents had fallen into

routine, sure, but what they'd had hadn't been anything close to what she'd wanted. So she'd made the crazy decision to marry Zacchaeus, but it hadn't brought her any closer to the life she wanted.

Yes, maybe it *was* time to accept that what she wanted just wasn't going to happen.

'Can I join you?'

Her heart thumped when she recognised Zacchaeus's voice. 'Sure.'

She found herself holding her breath again when he sat down beside her. And then she thought that she could hardly hold her breath the entire time Zacchaeus was there, and exhaled. But when she inhaled she inevitably got that masculine smell of his again. She steeled herself against it and found it easier to do now with a clear head.

At least that was what she told herself.

'It's a lovely evening,' he said, staring out over the stream.

'It is,' she replied, forcing herself not to look at him. But when the silence extended she asked, 'Did you just come out to tell me that?'

'No,' he said, and she waited. 'I wanted to apologise.'

Surprise had her eyebrows raising. 'Why?'

'Because I was a complete ass to you at supper and you didn't deserve it.'

She nodded. 'Thank you.' She bit her lip, contemplating whether she should say what was on her mind. Before she could stop herself, she did. 'Maybe you're right, Zacchaeus.'

'About what?'

'My expectations when I decided to come here.' She took a deep breath. Exhaled shakily. 'I think I made a mistake.'

'No, you didn't.' He angled towards her now, and she frowned. 'You made exactly the decision I would have made. In fact you've made the decision all of us would have made.'

'And that somehow makes it right?'

'For our kingdoms, yes.'

'And that's the most important thing, isn't it?'

'That's what we were taught.'

He shrugged, and something about the movement made her think he didn't like what they had been taught. She turned towards him and took his hand, ignoring the heat that went through her body.

'Tell me.' He turned his head and she felt something inside her quiver at what she saw there. 'Tell me what you can't tell anyone else. I promise it'll stay between us.'

She made the promise despite the voice in her head that told her she shouldn't. If what he told her would help Mattan and Aidara, she should tell Xavier and Leyna about it. But she knew she wouldn't.

Her free hand lifted to cup his face and she found herself moving closer. 'You aren't alone any more, Zacchaeus,' she whispered. 'Don't choose to be.'

Before she could stop herself, she leaned forward and kissed him.

Heat immediately seared her lips, and then softened to a sizzle that sent frissons of warmth through her body. Though he hadn't moved at first—and her heart had raced at the prospect of making such a terrible mistake—he leaned into the kiss now, nudging her lips open with his tongue so that they could taste each other.

She moaned as her tongue joined his and found

herself lost in sensations she'd never felt. She'd kissed men before. Her first had been an innocent curiosity that hadn't made her feel as if she'd missed anything. Her next had been with Josh, the boy she'd thought she would one day marry and who'd broken her heart. But even with him the kiss had never felt so…so *right*.

In fact, she felt cheated. Had she known kissing could feel so good she might have done it more. But then she thought that maybe it wasn't the act but the person she was doing it *with*.

And then she stopped thinking so that she could enjoy the way Zacchaeus kissed her as though she were the only woman alive.

She savoured the way her body had gone all tight and achy. The way it felt pleasure lined with a pain that didn't hurt but only served to tell her it wanted *more*.

And then there was the fact that she could finally enjoy the smell of him. The thought had her moving the hand that still held his to behind his neck, pulling him in closer so that she could go deeper.

But she felt a hand rest on the one she'd just

moved, gently removing its grip as Zacchaeus pulled back.

'Nalini,' he said, his voice gruff. 'We shouldn't be doing this.'

She blinked. 'Why not?'

'Because…because…' She waited as he tried to find an excuse. And then she realised *why* he was trying to find an excuse and felt her body go cold.

'It's fine, Zacchaeus—you don't have to make something up. I get it.' She shifted away from him and then stood and brushed the skirt of her dress.

'You get what?' he asked, standing up with her.

She fought against the sudden burn of tears in her eyes. Was he going to make her say it? The prospect of the humiliation had her standing a bit taller, and helped her ignore the tears.

'That you *want* to be alone,' she said, refusing to say the truth. That he hadn't wanted her as much as she'd wanted him. That perhaps he hadn't wanted her at all. And that she'd made yet another mistake when it had come to trusting a man.

'It's not that,' he replied, taking a step towards her. But he stopped when she shook her head.

'So you're saying that you're actually going to talk to me? That you're finally going to be honest?'

'I…' It was all he said and she shut her eyes briefly before speaking again.

'You're going to do this alone, aren't you?'

'I don't have a choice.'

'There's always a choice,' she replied, and realised she was speaking to herself just as much as she was to him. 'It's lonely ruling by yourself, Zacchaeus. Not only because you'll be doing it alone, but because it's hard work. It's *important* work. Having someone at your side, supporting you, helping you… It makes things a hell of a lot easier.'

'And what if you choose the wrong person?' he asked, his voice low and uncertain, a tone she'd never heard from him. 'That's worse, isn't it? Having someone at your side who's supposed to support and help you, but doesn't.'

'Are you worried that I would be like that?'

'I don't know you, Nalini. You could be.'

It stung but she merely told him, 'I'm not hiding who I am.'

'You're hiding something though. The real reason you're here.'

She opened her mouth to reply, but emotion had her clamping it closed again. Eventually, she said, 'I guess we're both not telling each other the whole truth then.'

But he wouldn't let it go. 'Is it because of your family?'

'Yes,' she replied, hoping that telling him that would be enough for them to move on.

'What about them?'

'They didn't want me here, and I chose to come. What does that say about what I left behind?' Because he looked as though he was going to push for more, she sighed. 'It's not rocket science. They don't think highly of you because of all that's happened. They didn't want me to marry you. So in coming here I've disobeyed them.' *Again.* 'Does that make more sense?'

He nodded. 'And you? What do you think about me?'

'Honestly?' she asked, and took the slight movement of his head as a yes. 'I don't know.

There are parts of you that I really like, and then there are others...' She trailed off, but saw that he understood.

'It's all a bit of a mess, isn't it?' He gave her a soft smile that had her heart beating against her chest like an insistent houseguest at the front door.

'Yes,' she agreed, and his smile got wider. For a moment. And then it slipped from his face, making her wish she could say something to bring it back.

'You're not wrong, you know. Things are a mess here. They have been for some time. And I'm a mess too, because of it.' He paused. 'You don't have to clean up this mess, Nalini.'

'I don't intend to,' she answered, though her heart told her she very much wanted to.

'So we'll keep this strictly—'

'Professional? In line with our business arrangement?' She didn't wait for his answer. 'That's fine.'

There was an awkward silence before she forced her legs to move. He fell into step beside her as they made their way back to the castle.

'Your mother and grandmother,' he said into

the quiet. 'They didn't come to see you off because you'd disobeyed them?'

Nalini thought back to when Zacchaeus had arrived at Mattan to take her to Kirtida. It had only been the day before, but the fogginess of the memory made it seem like months.

'Yes. Though, to be fair, they didn't really want to see you either.'

He laughed softly. 'That *is* fair.'

'Based on what they think they know about you, maybe so.' She regretted saying it before the last word left her mouth.

'But now you think differently?'

'I think that I can't go home,' she replied. 'But I can't keep doing this either.' She stopped walking and turned to face him. 'I want to make this work for both our kingdoms' sake—for *our* sake—but not if you're going to keep treating me the way you have been.'

'You're right.'

She hid her surprise. 'No more hot and cold, Zacchaeus.'

'I agree.'

'We respect each other.'

'Yes.' He paused. 'I'm sorry if I gave you the impression that I don't respect you. I do.'

'Thank you.'

They began to walk again.

'I mean it,' he said. 'And I know that—' he nodded his head to where they'd just kissed, and then rubbed the back of his neck '—complicated things.'

'It didn't,' she said brightly. 'We'll pretend it never happened.'

He looked unconvinced but nodded. 'So we'll keep doing our wedding appointments.'

'Yes.'

'And I'll behave at the next meal. We'll have a civil conversation, and you won't have to get drunk to survive it.'

'I wasn't—' She broke off when she saw the grin and felt her lips curve even as the butterflies fluttered from her chest down to her belly. 'A princess never gets drunk, Zacchaeus.'

'Of course not,' he said sombrely and stopped in front of the castle doors. 'And it's Zac.'

'What?'

'Call me Zac,' he repeated. 'I don't really go by Zacchaeus outside of my official duties.'

Inexplicably touched, she nodded. 'Zac it is.'

He smiled. 'Thanks. Rest well tonight.'

'You too,' she replied and returned to her room slightly dazed.

And was completely flabbergasted when she was greeted by an easel, paint and a stack of empty canvases against the wall.

CHAPTER SEVEN

'I'M SORRY, I didn't think to ask whether you'd be here.'

Zacchaeus had planned it that way. He would *just happen* to be having his breakfast in the place he knew Nalini would be having hers. So he'd had time to prepare his response—something along the lines of *Oh, it's fine* and *let's share breakfast anyway.* But the moment his gaze rested on her, there was no hope of reciting anything he'd prepared.

Not when he was desperately trying to keep his expression blank. Because if Nalini knew what he was thinking as he took in the striped shirt she'd paired with a green pencil skirt, she would run far, far away from him.

He swallowed, trying to soothe the sudden dryness in his throat. But the moment he did, he found his eyes travelling down the length of her—pausing at her hips to appreciate how her skirt highlighted the curves of them, and then on her legs which, paired with the heels she wore, looked pretty fantastic too—and his mouth would dry all over again.

When he dragged his eyes away from her body and settled them on her face he realised that it too had that effect on him. Her hair was tied in a bun at the top of her head with a few curls spiralling next to each temple, leaving her face perfectly clear of obstruction. Combined with her clothes, she looked like every sexy librarian fantasy he'd never known he'd had.

And would now never forget, he thought, and forced his thoughts out of the gutter.

'You don't have to apologise,' he said stiffly. 'I decided to come out here this morning.'

'In the name of civility, or because of the meal we're supposed to be sharing today?'

'Civility.'

Her eyes widened and she brought a hand to her chest. 'Are you saying you *want* to have more than one meal with me?'

The scandalised tone had his lips curving up. 'This *is* for civility, so perhaps in future we'll share more than one meal. But today...' He paused and wondered if he should tell her the truth. And then decided she would find out any-way. 'Today I'll be heading to Mattan to con-tinue the negotiations with your brother and Leyna.'

'Oh,' she replied, and the glimmer in her eyes faded.

'Do you want to come with me?' he offered, unsure of why he'd said it except for the fact that he really wanted to bring that light back. But she shook her head and the curls next to her face bounced with the movement.

'No, thank you.'

'Are you sure? You could see your—'

'No,' she interrupted sharply, the meekness in the tone she'd used to deny him the first time gone. There was a beat of silence and then she sighed. 'I just think that going home would... I think it would make things worse.'

'Things with your mother and grandmother or things here?'

'Likely both.' She gave him a small smile. 'It would probably be best for me to stay here and let things settle at home—on Mattan, I mean,' she said very deliberately. 'I'll use the time to explore the castle. To get to know my new home. And you being away should give me the chance to get to know the staff too, without them worrying too much about you.'

She said the last part cheekily but he didn't mind. It was fascinating watching her talk herself back into the happy mood she'd greeted him with. Again, he found himself admiring that optimism, though a part of him wondered how he would ever be able to match that in their marriage.

And then he had to remind himself that he wouldn't have to, since their marriage would be one of convenience only.

'It's so pretty out here,' Nalini said, interrupting his thoughts.

He followed her gaze and settled back in his chair to enjoy the view. He'd had the table set outside under a gazebo in the garden when she'd told him she would be coming to Kirtida. It had been an attempt to make her feel more comfortable, since he knew the way the sun spread across the castle garden in the morning could quieten all kinds of anxieties.

Now that he was sitting here though, watching

the way the yellow and orange light claimed the trees and flowers, he wondered why he hadn't done it sooner. For himself. Perhaps because he hadn't been thinking about ways to quiet anxieties before Nalini.

'The pictures will look good,' she said, and he forced himself not to frown at his unsettling thoughts. 'Unless Stefan uses the ones he took slyly when I fell into the stream.'

'He did that?'

'Unfortunately.' She sighed, but gave him a wink. 'Do you think a drenched Princess will still garner enough respect to become Queen?'

'If that Princess is you,' he heard himself say, but quickly continued before either of them could dwell on it. 'He's given us all the pictures though.' Zacchaeus pushed the unopened envelope that held the prints towards her. 'And he's put the ones he suggested we release at the front.'

She picked up the envelope but didn't open it. 'Was he really able to do it so quickly?'

'Apparently.' She nodded, but still her hands didn't move. 'Aren't you going to open it?'

Her eyes met his. 'Why didn't you?'

He struggled to find an answer, and frowned.

He'd told himself he'd wanted her to see them first. He'd wanted her opinion before he formed his own. So why couldn't he just tell her that?

'I think that's the reason I can't open it either,' she said, studying him. 'Ridiculous, isn't it?'

'That we don't know the reason we can't open an envelope?'

'That we both know the reason but neither of us want to say it aloud,' she corrected him quietly. And then, as though in defiance, she tore open the flap of the envelope and drew the pictures out, holding them gingerly in her hands as she set the envelope aside.

He kept his gaze on her face as she looked through them. He wasn't entirely sure why, when she'd made a neat stack of the ones she was done with on his side of the table. He could have easily picked them up, looked through them himself. But he couldn't bring himself to when her expression was so much more riveting to look at.

She was trying to keep it blank. And it worked, for the most part. Except he could clearly see she was at battle with herself, trying to hide her emotions from him just as she was feeling them. Then there were her eyes. He thought he'd be able to tell what those emotions were if he could read them. They were screaming, but somehow it felt as if they were doing so in another language.

His heart thudded when he realised how badly he wanted to be fluent in that language.

And then suddenly her face changed into an expression that had him holding his breath. She was staring at one of the pictures—had lifted it closer and he could see the way her hand shook. Her eyes met his and then quickly looked away, and instead of setting the picture down on the pile next to him she set it on the other side of her.

'You're not happy with them?' he asked, desperately wanting to know what she thought. And what had put that look on her face.

'No, no,' she said. 'They're beautiful. Official, a little romantic. Hopeful. I agree with the ones he's suggested we use.'

'But one of them has upset you.'

She shook her head but didn't look at him. 'It was just the picture of us in the stream. It's… it's a little embarrassing.'

'Can I see it?'

She wanted to say no, he could see. But he

knew—they both did—that saying no would undermine what she'd just told him. She picked up the photo again, her eyes flitting over it before she handed it to him. His heart hammered as he took it from her, though for the life of him he couldn't figure out why he was nervous about looking at a picture.

But as soon as he saw it he realised why.

It captured the moment they'd been laughing at her fall. They were both standing in the stream, Nalini's dress drenched, as predicted, with the stream only up to his shins. But neither of those facts was important. Their faces were. Or, more accurately, the expression on their faces—on *his* face. An expression he'd never seen before. He looked… He looked *happy.*

There was more too. A freedom, a lightness, that he now remembered the extent of. He'd never felt that way before, and now that he had evidence of it he couldn't keep ignoring that he had. He also couldn't ignore that he'd felt that way because of Nalini. Because of the freedom, the light, the happiness clear on *her* face in that picture too.

It reminded him of the way he'd felt when

they'd kissed the night before. The way he was desperately trying to ignore the feelings that kiss had stirred. Or how he was pretending that those feelings weren't the reason he'd hoped to spend time with her that morning.

'We should send these to Mattan,' he said, placing the picture on the stack next to him. Keeping his face blank of the carnage that picture had left inside him.

'That's a wonderful idea.' She'd abandoned the pictures and was now pouring herself some coffee. She smiled at him from behind her cup before she drank, but it didn't shine through her eyes like her smiles usually did. 'The people of Mattan were really happy about the prospect of our marriage. These photos will make things more official.'

'I hope so,' he replied softly, struggling for more words when he was fighting against the voice screaming in his head to bring back the glimmer in her eyes.

'It will.' She placed her hand over his—to comfort him, he realised, though not for the reason she thought—but snatched it away almost immediately. 'I also wanted to say thank you for the painting things you had sent to my room last night. It was very…thoughtful of you.'

'You're welcome.' He paused. 'Will you paint something for me?'

She laughed nervously. 'Oh, I don't think you want that. I'm not very good, remember?'

'So you say, except I'm not looking for a masterpiece. I'd just like something from you.'

Her face flushed. 'Don't say I didn't warn you once you get it.'

'I won't.'

She bit her lip and then smiled at him. 'So, tell me what I should be looking for during my exploration of my new home.'

He grinned and told her about the secrets of the centuries-old castle. She listened as attentively as he imagined she would to an important political matter. She made comments he knew meant she was listening, and asked questions whenever he paused. And, though he knew he wasn't the world's best storyteller, the look on Nalini's face almost convinced him that he was.

They were wonderful qualities to have as a queen, he thought. She'd make her people feel well loved, listened to, appreciated. It was so different to how his mother had dealt with her people—her *subjects*, he reminded himself of what she'd called them—that he couldn't help but compare the two women.

And then he worried that he was projecting what he *wanted* to see in Nalini onto her, instead of seeing who she really was. Much like he imagined his father had done when he had first married Zacchaeus's mother.

'Do you believe that your ancestor threw himself out of the tower's window to stop his love from leaving Kirtida?' Her voice was low, every feature of her face captured by the legend Zacchaeus had just told her.

'So the story goes,' he said mildly, telling himself to enjoy it—her—rather than think about his mother. Or his father. Or what their marriage had done to him. Or what their choices had left him to deal with now. 'But honestly, if it *is* true, I'm not sure I'd respect the man.'

'Why not?'

He shrugged. 'He killed himself for no reason.'

'No reason?' she repeated, shock claiming the lines of her face. 'It was out of *desperation*. He'd tried everything to show his love he cared about her, but still she didn't believe him. Not when her family had told her he was trouble. That he only wanted to marry her because of her family's wealth.'

He lifted his brows. 'Sounds familiar, doesn't it?'

'Some of it, perhaps,' she replied dryly. 'But we're not in love. They were.'

'And the way to show your love for someone is hurling yourself out of a tower and plunging to your death?'

'Oh, stop being so pessimistic!' she exclaimed. 'He wasn't jumping out of despair. He was jumping out of hope. Her boat was just below the tower's window. If he'd made it—'

'He would have broken every bone in his body.'

'But he could have survived.' She grinned. 'And she would have nursed him back to health and they'd have lived happily ever after.'

He shook his head. 'She'd left him, Nalini. She wouldn't have done that if she hadn't had her reasons.' But when he realised he was no longer talking about the legend he continued quickly. 'You're awfully hopeful, aren't you?'

'Positive, hopeful—' she lifted her shoulders '—they're pretty much the same thing.'

'Maybe,' he allowed. 'But yesterday you weren't hopeful. Yesterday you were being positive. Today? With this story? You're hopeful. I think it might be because you're a romantic.'

'Nonsense.' Her voice sounded forced.

'You don't think you're a romantic?'

'Don't you have to leave soon?'

'I…' His gaze caught his secretary's at the entrance of the castle right at that moment and Zacchaeus gave the man a slight nod. 'Yes, I do,' he told Nalini, but frowned when he thought she looked as though she'd shrunk into herself. 'Are you okay?'

'Oh, yes,' she said cheerfully. Again, it was forced and his frown deepened.

'Did I upset you somehow? I didn't—'

'I'm fine, Zac,' she replied, and for a moment he was distracted by the way his name—the one only his family used—sounded on her lips. 'Go, negotiate. Send my love to Xavier and Leyna.'

He studied her and realised he wouldn't get

anything more from her than that. At least not now. So he said goodbye and left for Mattan, making a mental note to ask her about it later.

CHAPTER EIGHT

NALINI SPENT THE rest of the day wandering around the castle, talking to the staff and pretending that morning hadn't happened.

She should have got a clue about how things were going to go the moment she'd seen Zacchaeus—*Zac*—sitting at that table. She should have got a clue when her stomach had flipped at how gorgeous he'd looked in his blue shirt and black trousers. At how her mind had chosen that moment to remind her how hot his kiss had been, or how she'd woken up in a sweat, her chest heaving and her body flushed at the dream she'd had where things hadn't *quite* ended the way they had the night before.

There were countless signs that things were getting slightly too personal between her and her future husband. Like the way she'd felt when she'd taken the envelope from him, knowing that neither of them had wanted to open it out of fear.

Fear that those pictures would spark with the attraction they clearly felt for one another. That the images would reveal the emotional connection they shared. That it would be evidence of everything, really, that they were hoping to ignore.

And, of course, it had been exactly that.

It didn't take a master in body language to tell her that there was something going on between them. Not when the pictures had captured moments when she'd been looking at him when he hadn't been looking at her, and vice versa. And in all those pictures it was clear that their marriage wasn't going to be simple. It wasn't going to be convenient. In fact, Nalini worried that what those pictures told her—what that feeling in her chest told her—was that their marriage was going to be very *inconvenient*.

The picture of them both in the stream confirmed it. Though it was completely unflattering in the traditional sense, it had an appeal she'd felt drawn to. Their guards were down, they were happy, comfortable, and all of it seemed to be *because* they were together. She'd seen Zacchaeus realise it when he'd held that picture in his hands too. And so she had immediately changed the subject so that they could get back to boring old breakfast instead of talking about it.

But breakfast hadn't been boring. She'd loved hearing stories about the castle and its legends. It was only when Zacchaeus had told her that she'd sounded hopeful—that she was a romantic—that she'd no longer wanted to have that conversation.

Those characteristics sounded too much like the Nalini who'd got herself into trouble. Who'd been such a believer in romance—who'd been so *hopeful*—that she'd followed her heart so that she could have an adventure in love. That she'd trusted a man—though now, when she looked back, she saw merely a boy—she shouldn't have trusted. She'd had her adventure turn into a nightmare, the consequences of which still motivated her decisions. Still had her wanting to prove that she'd learnt from her mistakes. To prove that she wasn't the old Nalini any more.

An *adventure* that clouded every decision she'd made since with doubt.

The uncertainty of it lurked in the recesses of her mind, waiting for her to let her guard down.

And she was afraid—terribly afraid—that her guard was down now, with Zacchaeus.

Fortunately, Zacchaeus hadn't pushed her about why she'd denied being hopeful. And she'd had the rest of the day to herself to build her guard back up. Talking to the castle's staff had been enlightening. Though they hadn't been willing to share much about their King—new or previous—they were open about their lives there. Tentative still, she sensed, about what Zacchaeus's rule would mean for them, but optimistic. She'd got the idea that things hadn't been entirely amazing under King Jaydon's rule, though none of them would confirm it when she asked.

Perhaps she would ask Zacchaeus when he returned, she considered, tilting her head as she studied the painting she was busy with. While she'd been exploring the castle, she'd come across the tower room from which Zacchaeus's ancestor had apparently thrown himself. Though the story of it alone inspired her, the windows, with their one-hundred-and-eighty-degree view of the sea, offered so much atmosphere and light that it was the perfect place to paint.

Shortly after she'd found it she'd changed into casual clothes, set up her canvas and started painting the man who'd supposedly given his life for love.

Which was why it made no sense that the picture she was currently looking at bore a striking resemblance to the man she was about to marry.

'They told me I'd find you here.' Zacchaeus's voice sounded from behind her and she swirled around, angling her body in front of the painting.

'You're back already?'

'Yes,' he replied, narrowing his eyes. 'It's evening, Nalini. How have you not noticed?'

She frowned and looked out of the window to see that he wasn't lying. Somehow, she must have switched on the light in the room because it shone brightly over her painting. Which, unfortunately, made it a lot harder to hide from the man currently staring at her as if she'd lost her mind.

'I must have lost track of time,' she said brightly. 'Were the negotiations productive?'

'We're onto the details now, which should mean we'll be able to wrap things up soon.' He took a step closer. 'Why are you trying to hide your painting from me?'

It took her a moment to find words to respond, but then she said, 'Because it's not done. And you know how us artists are.'

She turned the easel around quickly and then stepped back in front of it when he took another step towards her.

'I think you're lying.'

'I'm not,' she replied, and wondered if he heard the hysteria in her voice. 'It's not done.'

'Oh, I believe that part, but I don't think that's the reason you don't want to show it to me.'

She stepped in front of him when he took yet another step forward, and set a hand on his chest to keep him in place. When he looked down at her, those enthralling eyes almost made her forget why she was stopping him. And when the temperature in them rose she suddenly remembered that she was only wearing leggings and a spaghetti-strap top, having abandoned her oversized shirt in an attempt to stay cool hours ago.

'I…er…perhaps we should get ready for dinner,' she said hoarsely.

'Or,' he replied in a voice that rasped with sexiness, 'you could show me that painting.'

'No, I don't think—'

'Come on, Nalini,' he said, a slow, dangerous smile spreading across his face. 'I just want a peek. I promise I won't distract from your creative process.'

She blinked. Tried to form words. But, for the life of her, the only thing she could do was swallow, and she wasn't even doing *that* well.

'Please,' he whispered, and she thought she felt the words on her skin when it broke out in goosebumps. He lifted a hand, brushed his thumb over her lips, and her knees nearly buckled, causing her to lean against him. With that teasing smile still on his face, he wrapped an arm around her, steadying her while bringing her body closer against his.

'This…this isn't fair,' she managed to say.

'Not sure what you're talking about,' he replied, but the smile turned cocky.

Damn it, why did that make him even more irresistible?

'It's not going to work.'

'No?'

His arm tightened around her waist and the smile slipped from his face. She felt his heart thud against hers, and realised that he was no longer teasing. She told herself to move, but she was paralysed. Caught in his eyes, in his stare, in his smell.

She *wanted* to be, she realised, as the voice in her head shouted warnings at her. Reminding her what had happened the last time she'd felt something even remotely close to what she did now.

And realising that—realising that whatever was happening between her and Zacchaeus now couldn't be compared to what she'd felt with Josh—had her stepping back.

'Fine, you've got your way.' She fought to keep her tone light but it only highlighted the way her voice shook.

'Are you sure?' he asked, reserved now, the emotion and tension of the seconds before gone.

'Yes, please.'

She gestured to the painting and in that moment was sure she would have given him a kidney if he'd asked for it. Anything to save herself from the intensity of his gaze.

She stepped back as he turned the easel around, and now felt her heart hammer for completely different reasons. Perhaps if what had happened between them *hadn't* just happened she would have been able to pretend that she was really just afraid that her painting wasn't good.

But now she knew better. She knew that that painting would tell him more than anything she would actually say to him ever could.

As did his face, she realised, when he saw the painting.

She was by no means an artist, but as she looked at that painting she realised *it* was art. Because beyond the physical look of him—the striking, intimidating, handsome features of his face—the brush strokes had somehow captured the emotion she didn't think anyone else but her saw.

Including *him*, she thought, looking at the expression on his face.

'You can have it,' she heard her voice say. When he turned to look at her, she blushed furiously. 'I mean, if you want it, you can have it.'

'I'd love it,' he said quietly. 'You're very talented.'

'Oh, I—'

'Just say thank you,' he told her with a small smile, and then turned back to the painting, studying it for a moment longer. 'I've never seen myself this way. Is this how you see me?'

'It *is* you,' she said awkwardly.

'But it's not, too. I feel like this is…like it's a better version of me.'

'I wasn't trying to paint it that way, if that's what you're implying. In fact, I wasn't trying to paint you at all. It kind of just happened.'

His smile had widened when he turned back to her. 'What do you think that means?'

'That subconsciously I was thinking about your request for a painting and painted one of you? Or—' she considered, trying hard not to make this seem like a big deal '—you look a lot like your ancestor in my imagination. That's who I thought I was painting when I came here. With the legend fresh in my mind and the room being as beautiful as it is.'

'You were painting a dead man?'

'If you keep pushing me, then yes,' she said cheekily, sensing that he was coming out of the strange mood.

'I take the fact that you didn't notice the time of day means you haven't eaten yet?'

'You'd be right.'

She grabbed her shirt from the floor and quickly put it back on. When she turned back to him, she felt herself flush again at the look on his face. But she straightened her shoulders, determined not to feel embarrassed. Again. The number of times she'd felt that way in this room was beginning to make her feel self-conscious, and she was *not* a self-conscious person.

'So, do you want to have dinner together?' he asked.

'You mean…eat together? Again?'

He tilted his head, his lips curving. 'How long are you going to keep making that joke?'

'Well, since you actually agreed to have only *one* meal with me per day, I'm going to have to say a long, long time,' she teased. 'Maybe in thirty minutes? I need to take a shower.'

'See you in thirty minutes.'

She walked out of the room and turned back to see him looking at the picture again. It sent warmth through her. Not because she'd painted it—though there *was* that—but because she knew it had given him a new perspective on himself. Perhaps even the one he'd so vehemently denied the first time they'd spoken.

That happy glow stuck with her, but chilled slightly when she saw the wrapped gift on her bed. Its size told her that it was a picture of some sort, and with shaky fingers she tore the wrapping off.

And felt that glow disappear so quickly, so completely, she wasn't entirely sure it had ever existed.

CHAPTER NINE

ZACCHAEUS BANGED ON Nalini's door, feeling just as thunderous as the sound of his banging. And then she opened it and he felt all his anger and annoyance snap away.

Her face was pale, and the sunny demeanour she always carried with her gone. She was still in the leggings that had driven him crazy an hour ago, but the shirt she'd worn was now un-buttoned, hanging loosely from her shoulders.

'What happened?' she asked dully, and his stomach churned.

'I could ask you the same thing.' He made sure his tone held none of the alarm he felt. 'We were supposed to be having dinner.'

'I...' Awareness shone in her eyes. 'Did I miss it?'

He thought about the extra thirty minutes he'd waited for her, just in case she'd got caught up with something. And then he'd realised she had no intention of coming down and felt his mood turn so quickly that he hadn't given much thought to how striding to her door and hammering on it might have seemed.

Considering it now, he didn't even know what he would have told her *had* she been standing him up. All he knew was that he didn't want the progress they'd made that day to disappear, and he wasn't going to let her spoil it either.

But that didn't seem to be her intention at all.

'Yes, you missed it. Can I come in?'

She nodded wordlessly and he walked into her room, ignoring the strange intimacy of doing so. He looked around quickly, hoping for some clue as to her behaviour. But he only saw her things, and the painting he'd been asked to give her.

'I see they put the painting in your room. I was considering giving it to you when you came down for dinner, but I wasn't sure you'd agree to dinner at all.'

'Who gave it to you?'

'The painting?' He frowned. 'Xavier did. Though he said something about it being from your grandmother.'

'Of course,' she muttered, and shook her head.

'You don't like it?' He walked towards it, his eyes taking in the beach scene. He wasn't entirely sure why it would upset her, especially since the style suggested she'd been the one who'd painted it.

'It's not one of my favourites, no.'

'But…you painted it?'

'Yes. A long time ago.'

'And your grandmother wanted to…remind you of the beach? Does she know we have beaches here?' It was a lame attempt at a joke but he was beginning to feel a little desperate.

'She wanted to remind me about how wonderful my decisions have turned out in the past,' she said sourly. 'And how she'll—*they'll*—never see me in any other way. But I can't believe she actually did this.'

'Did what? I'm sorry—clearly I'm missing something.'

She looked at him now, and some of the misery cleared in her eyes. 'I'm sorry for missing dinner. We can go down now if you like?'

'I'd like to know what kept you from coming down in the first place.'

'Just this reminder of what being home entailed. I was missing home this morning, but clearly I was romanticising what it was like to actually be there.'

He stared at her. 'Are you going to tell me what this whole thing is about?'

'No,' she replied coolly. He took a moment to process the surprise, and then he clenched his jaw.

'So, our civility is only coming from my side then?'

'Civility being your willingness to have more than one meal with me?'

'I thought I was being civil the entire day.'

'Of which you'd spent what—two hours—with me?' She shook her head. 'You don't get to act righteous because you were willing to be decent for a few hours.'

'Are you being serious?'

'I think you should leave, Zacchaeus.' She walked to the door and pulled it open. Waited beside it.

He couldn't find the words to respond. Hell, he couldn't even process what was happening. Not really. Not since the woman who had the sweetest personality he knew was kicking him out of her room. Not when she was picking a fight with him.

The thought of it had him walking through the door, straight to his bedroom. It had been a rough day, but by the end of the negotiations that evening he'd felt positive. As if finally, things were going right for him.

He and Nalini were getting along well. Though there was still residual tension between them from their kiss, he figured they could live with it. And when he'd been teasing her in the tower room he'd thought that perhaps they could even have a little fun with it.

She'd completely taken the wind out of his sails with that painting. And though the emotions it had created in him had been difficult to identify—similar to what he'd felt that morning when he'd looked at the picture of the two of them—he'd recognised that most of them were positive. That it had felt *good* to see himself that way. In a way he hadn't thought existed.

It had him thinking about what it meant that Nalini thought about him that way. He'd ignored the warmth that had spread through him at that perspective and had instead settled on having dinner with her. And then this entire mess had happened, and now he was wondering whether he'd misinterpreted what had happened between them.

Between them?

What was he thinking? Perhaps *that* was the problem—thinking that there *could* be something between them. Thinking that there *was* something between them. So, instead of being disappointed about what had just happened, he should be grateful. Because though things were going well between them now, that could change. It probably would.

Hadn't his father warned him that it would? He'd told his father little of his plan to protect Kirtida, knowing what it would do to him if he knew the kingdom was in danger. But Zacchaeus *had* told Jaydon about his planned marriage to Nalini. And had given strengthening Kirtida's ties to the alliance as a reason.

His father had told him then that a marriage of convenience might not work out. That if he chose the wrong person it might turn out to have exactly the opposite effect of what he'd desired. That he might not be able to trust his convenient wife. Zacchaeus had known Jaydon's warning had come from his own experience. And he'd ignored it because of how different Nalini and Michelle had seemed.

Was he doubting that now? he suddenly asked himself. Did he now think they were similar because of Nalini's behaviour? His mother had always been selfish. And her last actions on Kirtida had proved that selfishness yet again.

Michelle had been having an affair with the vice-president of Macoa for as long as Zacchaeus could remember. His childhood had been filled with tension because of it, and he'd grown up with his only example of love a broken marriage held together flimsily by the tape of royalty.

For the life of him, he couldn't figure out why she had chosen to cut that tape *now*. Why had she asked his father for a divorce? Why the urgency? Why the threats?

Zacchaeus knew there was no way his father would survive if his mother asked for a divorce a second time. So he'd intercepted all Jaydon's communications, making sure that *if*—when?—his mother asked again, his father would never find out. He'd positioned his ships at Kirtida's shores in case that request came with an act of violence, and let Leyna and Xavier think that he'd done it to strong-arm them into agreeing to his terms.

So did he think that Nalini was selfish like his mother? Or did he just think that his father was right and he needed to be careful around her?

No, she wasn't selfish. She wouldn't be marrying him for the sake of her kingdom if she was. But she *was* hiding something. He'd known that since the day she'd arrived on Kirtida. Her behaviour this evening, over a *painting*, had proved it. Then there was the way she'd reacted when he'd called her a problem child, and again that morning when he'd called her a romantic…

She was hiding something, he thought again. And told himself that that was enough reason not to trust her. She might not be selfish like his mother, but whatever she was hiding… It might be something that made her more like his mother than he wanted to believe.

And if that were the case he couldn't afford to have feelings for her—of any kind. It would no doubt lead to more pain for him—and hadn't he already had enough pain to last a lifetime?

He wouldn't trust her, he told himself. Because if he did, and it turned out badly, where would that leave him?

But the next day Zacchaeus was *still* trying to convince himself of his conviction not to trust Nalini.

He'd spent most of his morning doing that. His discussions on Mattan had told him that he and Nalini were going to have to speed up their wedding planning efforts. The way things were going, he suspected the negotiations would end that week. And then the only thing he needed to do to protect his kingdom was marry Nalini.

He'd thought about it during a visit with his father. His heart had ached—just as it always did—to see his father's pale complexion. To hear his weak voice. And, like always, he ignored the feelings that pulsed just beneath that ache that had nothing to do with his father's illness and everything to do with the way his father had treated him.

But still he'd realised that it was unfair to compare his mother to Nalini. Even when his father warned him—again—that he shouldn't trust her, he didn't buy that the secret Nalini was keeping would reveal that she was manipulative or selfish like his mother.

Afterwards, he'd spoken to his secretary, asking him for an idea of all that still needed to be done before the wedding. He knew that he and Nalini had an appointment to select the wine and flowers from local providers that afternoon, but he wasn't entirely sure where that would put them progress-wise.

What his secretary had told him then confirmed what he'd been thinking that morning. That there was no way someone who had taken it upon herself to view the venue and church, who had decided on the décor for both, *and* who'd impressed all those she'd come across, could be like his mother.

And then, of course, there were the engagement photos that had been splashed across every newspaper in the kingdom. Including the one they'd both been so taken with the day before, of them in the stream. The photo that, according to his secretary, had set social media alight with comments about how human their King had looked.

By the time Zacchaeus went down to meet Nalini for their wedding appointment he knew that whatever she was hiding wasn't something that made her untrustworthy. But it *was* something that had affected her badly, and he was determined to find out what it was.

CHAPTER TEN

SHE SHOULD APOLOGISE. She'd wanted to, almost immediately after she'd kicked him out, but then she'd remembered *why* she'd kicked him out and had kept her mouth shut.

But now that they were in a car together, ignoring the urge to apologise was a lot harder.

'You had a busy day today.' Zacchaeus broke the silence that had been between them since they'd greeted each other before heading for the wedding planning appointment.

'I wanted to get a head start.'

'Good idea, since we're almost done with the negotiations.'

She waited for the panic to take over, but it was nowhere near as intense as she'd expected. 'Things are moving a lot quicker than I thought they would.'

'Nervous?'

'No. You?' He gave her a look, and she nodded. 'Of course not. You're the one who wanted to get married in the first place. Why would you be nervous?'

It sounded a lot like babbling to her. But then she *was* nervous, though it wasn't about the wedding. At least, not entirely about that. The tension—caused by her actions, she knew—was making her anxious. And the longer it extended, the more she wanted to blurt out why she'd been so awful to him the night before, and the more she wanted to apologise.

But somehow neither of those two things seemed like the right thing to do. No, now she just wanted to get through this damn appointment and return to the safety of the castle. Where she could lock her door and pretend she hadn't let her grandmother spoil yet another thing for her.

And that it hadn't completely destroyed the hope she'd somehow *still* had of her family seeing her differently.

She was distracted when the car slowed down in front of a long row of shops. They had clearly been preparing for the King's visit—Kirtida's national flag hung from every lamppost on the street, and posters of Zacchaeus's coronation plastered in the windows. A small crowd had gathered once the car had stopped, and it took Nalini a moment to realise that the group was mostly female. And that the females were wearing T-shirts that had Zacchaeus's face printed on them…

'I think I've been misinformed about the way your people see you,' she said, and felt her smile grow as she watched one woman grip her friend's hand and do a jump.

He followed her gaze and winced. 'I'm not sure how they always know where I am.'

'Always?' she repeated. 'They?'

Now he grimaced. 'My…fan club, I suppose you could call them.'

Her mouth dropped. 'That's an actual thing?'

'Apparently.' He gave an impatient shrug. 'It's not like I created the group. Or approve of them. They just…kind of… *appear* where I am. Wearing—' he gestured towards them '—*that.*'

'So, if I understand you correctly,' she said in a mock serious tone, 'Kirtida's dark and mysterious King has a fan club of women who wear his face on their chests?'

'Oh, come on, don't say it like that.'

'Like what?'

'Like…like me being dark and mysterious is a thing. Or like my face is actually on their chests.'

She didn't reply, only lifted her eyebrows and nodded to where the group of women were proving his protests wrong.

'Yes, okay, fine. They like me. But it's just a thing that some women do.' Her eyebrows went higher and she had the pleasure of seeing her dark and broody future husband blush. It was charming. 'I don't mean it like that. I just—'

'I know what you meant,' she replied, and ran her tongue over her teeth. 'Do you have shares in the company that provides your face on clothing? Because I think it could look quite lovely on a veil if it's done in the right way.'

'Nalini, you know— Oh, you were joking.' He frowned. 'Is this going to be a thing now? You, teasing me about this?'

'Oh, definitely,' she replied and smiled at him. He returned the gesture and for a moment she forgot about what had happened the night before.

For a moment she allowed herself to be lost in his magnetic eyes. The ones that, the longer she looked into them, told her the darkness her grandmother had once warned her about had been caused by something incredibly difficult for him.

And, heaven help her, because she wanted to find out what it was. She *wanted* to fix him—the *mess* of him, as he'd called it—even though she knew she shouldn't.

The thought had her asking whether they should get out of the car, and immediately the spell was broken. When she joined him outside, she saw that the line of shops wasn't where they would view the flowers or taste the wine.

No, that place had somehow been obscured by the group of now screaming women.

She couldn't stop the giggle when she saw the horror on Zacchaeus's face, but took his hand as they walked through the throng of people to an amateur street festival set up for their benefit. Now that she saw it, she didn't know how she'd missed it.

Her eyes fluttered to the woman next to her—and to her T-shirt—and told herself *that* was why. Because those T-shirts *were* distracting. Just like the face on them was.

She shook it off and sighed in relief when they reached the first stalls. *This* she could do. This was what she'd been trained for. So she said the right things as she looked at the flowers, and drank from the wines carefully, being sure not to swallow anything lest she lose her head again. She greeted children and smiled as the crowd grew larger and a group of musicians—heaven only knew where they'd got their instruments from at such short notice—began to play.

The amateur street festival was becoming a lot more professional, she thought, and found herself enjoying the happy atmosphere. But she also had to acknowledge that a part of that was because she was finally getting to see Zacchaeus as King.

Of course she'd witnessed that already. She'd been dealing with the King from the moment she'd arrived. But it was different to watch him interact with his people. Not because he changed from who he was—he remained the careful, intent man she'd got to know. No, it was more because that deliberate seriousness was surprisingly charming.

It meant that each person felt as though they

were the centre of Zacchaeus's attention. As if their concerns were the only ones he had to deal with. As if the flowers he was looking at, or the wine he was tasting, were the best he'd ever seen, ever tasted.

It reminded Nalini of how she'd felt during their kiss. As if she'd been the only woman he'd ever wanted to kiss. As if somehow she was the centre of his universe.

The memory of it sent a flush through her and she grabbed a cold bottle of water from an ice bucket close by and pressed it to her cheek. She felt a tug on her hand then, and looked down into the biggest, bluest eyes she'd ever seen. Her heart already melting, she crouched down so that she could be level with the little girl who had taken her hand, and gave a smile to her mother before aiming it at the girl.

'Hi,' came a soft voice.

'Hello,' Nalini replied. 'Are you here with your mum?'

The girl nodded, but gave no other response.

'Are you here…to see the King?' Nalini tried again and this time the girl's eyes widened and a pretty pink covered her cheeks. Nalini's smile broadened as she realised what she'd been sin-gled out of the crowd for. 'I'll see what I can do.'

She winked at the girl, nodded at the 'thank you' her mother mouthed and followed the path her guards created so that she could find her way back to Zaccheaus.

'I'm sorry to interrupt,' Nalini said when she reached his side, and she saw a spark of grati-tude in his eyes when he turned away from yet another young woman.

'No, don't worry. We were just ending the conversation.' He smiled at the woman—whose crestfallen expression immediately brightened—and gestured for Nalini to start walking. 'What can I do for you?'

'Oh, it really isn't what you can do for me, but more about what you can do for one of your fans.'

'I don't think I have it in me to do another thing for one of my fans.'

'No, you do,' she corrected. 'At least you will for this one.'

She stopped in front of the young girl and her mother—both of whom looked suitably im-pressed that she'd been able to get Zaccheaus there. She didn't ponder why—did they not think she'd be able to get the man she was about to marry to talk to them?—and instead focused on the way Zacchaeus had done the same thing she had earlier, and was now crouched in front of the girl.

'Hi, there,' Zacchaeus said.

Shy, the girl slipped behind her mother's leg, and the woman immediately went red and started to apologise.

'There's no need,' Zacchaeus said. 'It's hard for me to talk to people too, sometimes.' He directed his next words to the girl. 'It's scary, isn't it?' She nodded and angled her body slightly more towards him. 'But sometimes people aren't as scary as they look.' He whispered something in the girl's ear and she giggled.

Watching it sent a punch through Nalini's heart and she nearly staggered backwards. Instead, she smiled at the girl and her mother and slowly moved away from them, feigning interest in the flowers at a stall she'd already seen to make her disappearance less obvious. She kept moving then, through the people, offering smiles, shaking hands.

But, determinedly, she made it back to the car and thanked the heavens that her bodyguards would make sure she had privacy.

She wasn't sure why it had shaken her so much. No, that was a lie. She *did* know. And perhaps knowing had shaken her even more. Because she could see a future with a little girl in it. With little boys too, and maybe even some pets. And in that future she and Zacchaeus were those children's parents, and those pets' carers.

She didn't want to be thinking of their future together. But she was and that meant that she was slipping back again. Back into the girl who made plans for her future. Stupid, romantic plans that would never, ever come true. Plans that were idealistic, and only proved that she was naïve. And that she wasn't someone who made good choices.

She knew better than to do that again. She knew better than to blindly trust a man, and make plans for a future together. It didn't matter that she felt as if she knew him better than she'd ever known Josh. Or that the inner voice that had warned her about Josh—that she'd only realised she'd ignored *after* the beach incident—was seemingly quiet about Zacchaeus.

Nalini had sworn she wouldn't go back to being that girl. And she'd chosen to obey her family to prevent that. But after her grandmother had sent her that painting, Nalini could see where she stood with them now. In their eyes, she'd disobeyed them again. And she was finally beginning to realise that, no matter what she did, it wouldn't change the way they thought of her.

So she couldn't go back to Mattan. She had to stay here with Zacchaeus and face the decision she'd made. She tried to focus on the fact that that decision hadn't only been made to prove her family wrong. She'd wanted to save her kingdom too—she *was* saving her kingdom. Because if she didn't focus on that she would have to face the doubt she felt about her decision.

A decision she sensed would do more damage than the one she'd made with Josh…

Damn it, she *hated* this uncertainty. Hated it that the painting hadn't only shown her that her family's perception of her wouldn't change, but that it had actually done what her grandmother had intended. She couldn't deny that it had. Not when that painting had really been a reminder *from* herself *for* herself. A reminder that she should be careful. That she should make sure she could really trust someone before she did anything.

She didn't know if she could trust Zacchaeus. Not with certainty. And she only had to remember the last time she'd taken a chance to know that she *needed* certainty. She only had to remember how she'd trusted the man who had led her down to the beach that day. Who had kissed her as they'd walked down the path from the castle, and giggled with her as they'd tried to avoid the castle guards.

The man who'd then mocked her when she'd called out for his help as his friends pulled at her clothing, her jewels.

She shut her eyes tight, hoping it would stop the memories. But then told herself to embrace the memories. To let them fortify the part of her that had softened watching Zacchaeus today. She'd known that kind man had existed inside him. And though he'd tried to deny it—to hide it—he couldn't keep that from her any more.

But that didn't mean the King beneath that kind man didn't exist. Until she was completely sure of it, she couldn't trust him. She needed to protect herself. And protecting herself meant that she couldn't trust her own judgement either.

'Nalini?'

She opened her eyes just in time to see Zacchaeus settle inside the car.

'Done?'

'So it seems,' he said evenly. 'Which tends to happen when my fiancée disappears from our wedding appointment.'

'The wedding appointment was long over, Zacchaeus,' she replied in the same tone. 'We saw all the flowers, tasted all the wine in the first two hours. The last few were really just for the sake of your image. To memorialise the people out and about with their King. I saw the photographers,' she said when his forehead creased.

'I didn't know anything about that.'

'I know,' she said, softening her tone. 'It was probably some scheme from your advisors. Hence the fact that this simple appointment turned into a full-on parade.'

'Is that why you left?'

'No, it's not.' But she had no intention of telling him why she had. 'Perhaps we should head back to the castle now?'

CHAPTER ELEVEN

ZACCHAEUS WASN'T SURE his plan would work.

Especially after that afternoon, when things had shifted between ease and tension, closeness and distance with him and Nalini. But still he'd told himself to give his plan a chance.

Which was why he was standing at the edge of the beach that stretched out in front of the castle, waiting for Nalini.

'I think I'm in the wrong place,' came her voice from behind him, and when he turned Zacchaeus heard the soft intake of his own breath.

What was it about the way she wore a dress that had him feeling this way? He knew she didn't intend to do it to him. Not when it was a simple Grecian-style dress that fell to her ankles from a high neckline. She'd let her hair down this evening, but her face was clear of make-up, and he wondered why he thought that she was trying but not trying at the same time.

It was more than likely the latter, he thought. Especially after he'd had to remind her about their deal—the one *she'd* insisted on—to share one meal per day. After *he'd* had to insist when she'd brushed it off, claiming that she was tired. Even if he did believe her, he wouldn't have agreed anyway. He wanted to know why she'd left him during their appointment that afternoon. And why she'd kicked him out the day before.

Was it so wrong that he'd ensured the intimacy, the privacy, of dinner to do so?

'You're not in the wrong place,' he told her. 'This is where we're having dinner tonight.'

'Are you sure? Because I don't see a table anywhere. And the candles—' she gestured to the pathway that was lined with candles '—seem a lot more appropriate for a date than a forced dinner.'

'Aren't they the same thing?' he asked easily. 'I've seen plenty of movies where dates look a lot less comfortable than what we share.'

'Which movies are you watching?' She shook her head in disgust and he took her hand, hiding his smile at the fact that he'd successfully distracted her. 'You've been on dates before. Surely you know that our dinners—or meals—aren't comparable to real dates?'

'I'm not sure that I do. I've never really been on a date before.'

'That can't be true.'

He heard the surprise but it didn't bother him. He was quite enjoying their walk down the beach path that would eventually take them to where they'd be having dinner.

'But it is.'

'Even though the "I love Zacchaeus fan club" exists?'

He chuckled. 'Probably *especially* because it exists.' He paused, considering her question more carefully. 'I think you're mistaking the fact that I haven't gone on a date with the fact that I haven't dated. I *have* dated. Women have come to the castle—appropriate women from appropriate families—and we've spent time together.'

She stopped next to him. 'You think that's dating?'

'For us, yes.'

'Maybe that's true,' she said, and started walking again. 'But it sounds terrible.'

He let out a surprised laugh. 'So you're saying things weren't like that for you?'

'No,' came the sombre reply, and he could sense the shift in her mood again. But then she said, 'I haven't really dated either. The real kind or the kind you're talking about.'

'So I was your first kiss?' he teased, and frowned when she didn't respond immediately. Her soft reply had his heart racing uncomfortably in his chest.

'Yes, you were.' She bit her lip. 'Is that really how it's supposed to be? I mean is it…is it always that…that *wet*?'

She blinked innocently at him and he felt his eyes widen. And then her face transformed and she burst out laughing. It took him a moment to realise that she'd been pulling his leg, and another to see the humour in it.

And then he found himself smiling too. Before long, his laughter joined hers and for the second time in as many days Zacchaeus found himself wiping tears from his eyes at a joke.

'You are *so* naïve,' she said, her finger brushing a tear from her cheek. 'And so *proper*. It's adorable that you think kissing should only happen if you're dating.'

'That's not—' He broke off at her smile and before he could help it he was smiling back. 'I'll get you back for that.'

'I'd be disappointed if you didn't,' she said, her eyes twinkling.

And suddenly he was thinking that things felt like before between them. Like the day they'd almost been friends, and not whatever they were now. He stopped walking when he realised they'd made it, and turned to her.

'We're here,' he said softly, and watched the surprise on her face as her gaze shifted to behind him. Some might have said he'd overdone it—*he'd* told himself as much when he'd been planning it. But the look on her face made it worth it.

She was surprised, sure, but there was more on the beautiful features of her face. She was impressed, a little touched, and the slightest bit overwhelmed. And though he was getting better at reading her, he knew there was more still. He wished he could read it all. All the secrets those features held.

But when her eyes met his again he realised

that though he couldn't identify every emotion on her face, he *felt* them. Because his heart had immediately pulsed when she'd looked at him. The awareness he always felt around her had hummed louder in his body. And now his fingers itched—to brush away the hair the slight breeze had brought across her forehead. To brush those full pink lips and see them part for him.

Under the moonlight, he felt utterly captivated by her. As if she'd put a spell on him, and that spell demanded he kiss her. That he taste the sweetness of her mouth again, and perhaps get a touch of that fire of her tongue too.

'It's lovely,' she said, breaking the spell as she took a step back.

He nodded and cleared his throat. 'I thought we could do something nice for a change.'

'Well, it certainly is nice. Shall we?'

She didn't look at him as they walked to the large rock he'd arranged for their dinner to be served on. It was on the other side of the beach, surrounded by smaller rocks, and high enough that the waves merely crashed against it, not engulfing it like it did the others. He hoisted himself up and ignored the hand she gave him.

Instead, he put his hands on her waist and lifted, biting back the smile when he saw her eyes widen as he set her down.

'Was that your way of showing me how manly you are?'

'Only if it worked,' he said mildly. He waited a few seconds and then asked, 'Did it?'

He loved the way her eyes crinkled as she laughed at him, and his chest filled with an emotion he didn't recognise. 'Yes, it did. But I'll never admit it aloud again.'

'Once is enough,' he replied cheekily, and winked when she shot him a look. 'I wanted us to have some privacy, so there won't be anyone serving us dinner.' He gestured to the basket next to them. 'But we have enough food in here to feed an army, and wine. Just in case you need it,' he said with a smile.

She gave him a small one back, but it sobered quickly. 'Why do we need privacy?'

'Because I was hoping we could talk.'

He saw her stiffen. 'About?'

'About what's been happening between us the last few days. I'm sorry but… I've missed something, and I'd really love to know what.'

'You haven't missed anything.' Her hands fiddled with the napkin in front of her. 'I've just been…reminded of why I'm here.'

'By your grandmother?'

'No, by myself.'

'Because you painted that picture.'

'Yes.'

'Why? When?'

'Why did you overthrow your father, Zacchaeus?' she shot back suddenly. When he didn't answer her, she threw her hands up. 'See? There are things neither of us want to talk about. So, since we don't need privacy because we're not going to be having this conversation, we can—'

'He's ill, Nalini,' he interrupted quietly, knowing that if he wanted her to trust him—if he wanted to trust *her*—he had to give them both a reason. 'He couldn't rule any more, so we came up with this…this *plan* to say that I'd overthrown him.' He fell silent. 'It was his idea. He didn't want people to think that he was weak.' *One person in particular*, he thought, but didn't say it.

A stunned silence stretched over them and eventually she said, 'So the rumours were true.'

'I didn't realise they'd reached Mattan.'

'They were whispers, really. And so ridiculous that we didn't pay them much heed.' She paused. 'Why would you need to hide that he's ill? Illness isn't weakness.'

'To my father it is.'

'But being overthrown isn't?'

'He thought that if I was the one who was overthrowing him, it wouldn't be so bad. It would make me seem powerful, more ruthless, and he would merely look like the father who had given in.'

'Based on what?' she asked. 'There was no military involvement. My understanding of it was that you forced him off the throne through guerrilla methods. Getting the support of the powerful in the kingdom. Ousting him, essentially.'

'Yes.' He shrugged. 'That's what we told people.'

'And they believed you?' She frowned. 'How could they? Wouldn't you have needed actual support? Wouldn't your inner circle have to know? Do they?'

'We did have actual support. When we came up with this plan, my advisors—who were also my father's advisors—started laying the foundation for the coup. They started whispers of rash decision-making, decisions that weren't entirely in the interest of the kingdom. There was more, of course. But…it wasn't that hard, really.'

He shifted when he saw how she was looking at him, but she merely said, 'So your advisors know he's ill?'

'They know he wanted to step down. And because they're the most loyal people I know, they did exactly as they were asked without much questioning.' He tilted his head and then nodded. 'But I think they know.'

She pursed her lips and reached for the bottle of water in front of her. After she'd taken a sip, she set it down again and settled back in her seat. 'Why did you go along with it?'

'Why…' He trailed off. 'What do you mean?'

'You knew how this would make you look. And *you* didn't want to be ruthless and powerful. That's not how you wanted to be seen as King. So why would you go along with it?'

His mouth dried completely. He took a drink of his own water and cleared his throat, but neither of those things worked. He wasn't sure he could voice an answer. And even if he could find his voice, he wouldn't have the words to answer anyway.

How had she seen through everything he'd just told her? How had she seen through it to *him*? Why did she even care? No one had asked for his opinion. His father had just *told* him what would happen, and had left him to fall in line. There had been no discussion regarding his feelings, and perhaps that had been part of the reason he'd been ignoring them.

Until now.

Until *Nalini* was asking him about it.

'I was…helpless not to,' he said in a hoarse voice, surprising himself. 'It wasn't a suggestion. It was a command.'

'Much like the reason I'm here?' she asked lightly, and the left side of his mouth lifted.

'I suppose.'

She nodded. 'Which means you still had a choice, though you felt like you didn't. You still had that choice. *You* chose to go along. Why?'

'Why did you choose to come here?'

Annoyance flashed in her eyes, but he saw

that it covered hurt. He clenched his fist to keep from reaching out to her.

'I came here for my kingdom.'

'Nalini—'

But she lifted a hand, silencing him. 'I came here for my kingdom, but for myself too. I couldn't keep living on Mattan. Not when the life I was living there was destroying every good thing about me.'

CHAPTER TWELVE

'DRAMATIC, AREN'T I?' Nalini said, trying to poke fun at herself. No, she thought. She was trying to make telling him the real reason she'd agreed to marry him seem less severe in her mind.

'Considering what I know about your family, it doesn't really sound that dramatic at all.'

'They're not terrible people,' she said immediately and closed her eyes, wondering why she always felt the need to defend her grandmother and mother's behaviour.

'I'm sure that's true,' Zacchaeus said when she opened her eyes again, his own eyes filled with compassion. 'But families are complicated. Royal families more so. And sometimes what they do...' A shadow, dark and haunting, crossed his face. 'Sometimes what they do *is* terrible. And sometimes *they* can be terrible too.'

'You're not talking about my family now, though, are you?'

'No,' he replied. 'But I would like to know what they did to make you feel this way.'

Should she tell him? He already knew more than she'd ever intended to let him know. But somehow telling him about Josh didn't feel right.

Her gaze met his, and once again she was hit with the compassion in his eyes. She wondered why it was so captivating. Was it because it was so unexpected? Or perhaps because it took away that dark look always lurking in his eyes?

Caught off guard, she spoke before even realising it. 'When I was seventeen, I did something a little…irresponsible.'

She thought about the details, about how she'd got to the beach that day, and couldn't find any words that wouldn't make her seem like some stupid, naïve teenager. She ignored the voice in her head telling her that she had been.

'I was always more rebellious than Xavier and Alika,' she continued, settling on telling him about everything but *that day*. 'And after that thing happened it cemented the way my parents saw me. They used it to make sure I knew my place.'

'Which was firmly under their thumb?'

'Yes. And I… I'd learnt my lesson, so I had no interest in venturing out again. I did everything they'd ask—everything to try and prove to them I wasn't the person they thought I was. Not any more.'

'Like choosing to marry a man you don't know to save your kingdom?'

Instead of being shocked at how much he saw, she nodded. 'But it's pointless. They'll never see me as someone other than the irresponsible person they think I am. Of course, I've only just realised it. With that painting.' She gave him a moment to put the pieces together, and then continued. 'But I also chose to come here because the more time I spent doing exactly what my parents wanted—and then, when my father died, doing what my mother and grandmother wanted—the more the person I was disappeared.'

'The person who snuck homeless kittens under her jacket to take back home to the castle?'

Her lips curved. 'I'd forgotten about that.'

'How could you?' he asked with a smile of his own. 'Don't you still have the scars?'

Now she laughed, even as her hand fluttered up to her chest. 'Fortunately, all evidence of scratches disappeared a few months after that.' She tilted her head. 'How did you know? I was pretty stealthy, even if I do say so myself.'

'You were,' he agreed. 'But since I'd pretty much had the same idea, I'd been watching the kittens, waiting for the right moment to get them. Considering it was the New Year's Day parade on Mattan, and we were there as a part of our "royal duties"—' he lifted his fingers for air quotes '—I couldn't just run from my father's side as I wanted to.'

'We were children,' she replied, rolling her eyes. 'We should have been able to save the damn kittens if we wanted to.' She bit her lip. 'I'm sorry, that wasn't very princess-like of me.'

A sexy smile widened his mouth, and she felt the same butterflies in her stomach as when they'd been caught in each other's gazes earlier. 'Let's make a deal. You never have to be princess-like around me.'

'Are you sure?' she replied in a low voice,

vaguely wondering where this flirtatiousness was coming from considering they'd just spilled their deepest secrets to one another. 'Because I can be *pretty* unroyal.'

'Really?' Interest sparked in his eyes. 'Tell me more?'

'Well, once, after I'd been dancing with this guy all night at a royal ball—' she lowered her voice even more, leaned forward '—I asked if he wanted to go back to—' she was almost purring now '—the kitchen with me to get some of the dessert we'd missed.'

He blinked, and then a deep rumble of laughter spilled out from his throat. 'What did he say?'

'After the disgusted look he gave me, he said no.' She lifted her shoulders. 'So I went alone. And really, it was his loss. The tiramisu was delicious.'

'You're really something else, aren't you?'

'I can unequivocally say yes to that. Is it going to be a problem?'

His eyes turned serious so quickly her heart stalled. 'Not for me, no.'

Now her heart twisted. 'Good.'

They smiled at each other, and she ignored all

of the thoughts in her mind. The ones wondering at how easy things could be between them at times. How tense at others. How there was always this attraction—that pull—she felt for him.

If she thought about it, she would be tempted to wonder what it meant. Or why she always, always found herself wanting more of him, regardless of where they'd left things.

'What happened to those kittens, by the way?'

'They all went to loving homes in the kingdom.'

'You didn't get to keep one?'

'"A castle is not the place for a *pet*",' she said in the same tone of voice her mother had used on her years ago.

'Wow.' He shook his head. 'That's almost exactly the same thing my mother told me when I asked her whether I could take the kittens.'

'*That's* why you didn't get them?'

He nodded. 'Though I probably would have taken them anyway. Except when I got there they were gone and all I could see was you in a wildly moving jacket.'

She chuckled. 'You believe castles can have pets, don't you?'

'Of course.'

'Great. But, to be honest, I doubt your opinion would have mattered much to me. I would have just let the kids get them anyway.'

She froze immediately, the apology on the tip of her tongue. But she couldn't say it because that would entail her admitting that she'd said something inappropriate. For all she knew, he might not have picked up that she'd—

No, she thought as she saw his face. He'd definitely heard her slip.

'Sorry,' she said, wincing. 'That was a bit strange, wasn't it?'

'A little,' he admitted. 'But not untrue.'

Her cheeks grew hot. 'I suppose.'

'Are you embarrassed that we're going to have a child together? Excuse me,' he added slyly, '*children*.'

'I'm *not* embarrassed. It's just…strange.'

'Not *that* strange though,' he said, and she could hear that teasing lilt to his voice. 'I mean, we *are* going to be married. And we're royal, so we need to provide Kirtida with an heir.'

'Don't get cocky with me,' she warned. 'I know what this marriage entails.'

'Oh, I don't think that you do.'

She bit her tongue, knowing what he was trying to do. And then realised that she could play at his game too.

'Maybe you're right,' she said softly. 'What does marriage entail? Is it…is it like that kiss we shared? You know, my *first* kiss.'

Appreciation lit his face and he gave her a lazy smile. 'It's a lot like that, but a little…more.'

She almost laughed, but found that her breath was strangled.

'It's okay,' he added. 'You don't have to be scared.'

Now she did laugh—and heard it as a gasp for air. 'I'm not *scared*.'

'Are you sure? Because you're acting like you are.'

'I'm not scared,' she said, and for the life of her she didn't know what prompted her to get up, saunter over to Zacchaeus and sit down on his lap. She saw the way his eyes widened, but didn't give herself a chance to see it as a warning. Instead, she lowered her head to his and repeated, 'I'm not scared'.

And kissed him.

* * *

He'd enjoyed teasing her. He'd loved the way her cheeks had turned pink with only the candles and moon bringing light to them. And the way she'd been adamantly trying to deny that she wasn't fazed by the prospect of the physical side of their relationship.

Perhaps if *he* hadn't been as affected by her casual reference to their children some day—the reference that reminded him of *how* those children would get there—he wouldn't have kept pushing. But, because he had, she was now on his lap, making it perfectly clear how she felt.

And those feelings were anything *but* fear.

Someone who was scared would not be kissing him with so much passion, so much heat, that he worried he was no longer breathing. But what did breathing matter when he could taste the fire he'd wondered about earlier? Fire that burned his lips, his mouth, that set his entire body ablaze?

His arms went around her waist, pulling her closer so that he could feel her body against his as their tongues met, duelled. But her position on his lap was too awkward and he broke their contact to lift her dress, drawing one leg over his own so that she straddled him.

She gave him a lazy smile that had the temperature of his body soaring even higher, before dipping her head to return to what they'd been doing. He wasn't entirely sure what was happening—how he had the woman he'd demanded marry him kissing him—but he didn't care. He was much too taken by how she captivated his every sense.

How his eyes, though closed, still saw her sexy smile. How his ears heard her tiny little moans, a stark contrast to the crashing of the waves against the rocks. How she tasted sweet and fiery at the same time, how her smell mingled with the sea, the most intoxicating scent he'd ever been offered in his life.

And then there was the feel of her.

He thought he was in heaven as he ran his hands up the thighs exposed to him now. But the thrill—the indecency—of it told him it was more than likely hell. Tempting him to rip off the dress that kept the softness of her magnificent skin from him. Taunting him with what he could feel—the curve of her waist, the softness of her breasts—because now he knew exactly how they felt in his hands. And how much better they would feel without her dress covering them.

He stood then, holding her with one arm and using the other to clear the table before setting her down on it. He ignored the crash of the plates, utensils and whatever else was on the damn table, and instead focused on how laying her down changed the dynamics between them.

He could deepen their kiss now, and give her just as much as she wanted. And take just as much as *he* wanted. He could break the contact of their mouths to run his lips down the slender column of her neck. His hand settled on her breast as his lips suckled, kissed, *claimed* every piece of skin he could access, but still he wanted more. He ran his hand down her side and up her dress...

And froze when a chilly wave crashed down on them.

There was a stunned silence as they both processed what had just happened, and when he opened his eyes he saw the surprise on Nalini's face. He watched as her eyes widened and closed again, and in that brief second realised it meant they were about to get a repeat performance.

Not that bracing for it helped. The wave was just as chilly, just as surprising. But it spurred him into action and he moved quickly, jumping off the rock before lifting his arms to help Nalini down too. They barely missed the third wave and he took her hand, leading her back up the beach, away from the water.

'Well,' was all he managed as he looked down at himself.

His clothes clung to his body, his shoes completely drenched. He took a moment to appreciate that the unexpectedness of the wave had settled his arousal too, saving him from the potential embarrassment of having to face it now that they were no longer in the throes of passion.

He turned to her and saw that she hadn't fared any better. Though he wouldn't complain. Not when her white dress was now transparent, and plastered to the body he'd got to enjoy only a few minutes ago.

'Well, indeed,' she said finally, and her eyes met his.

Barely a second had passed before they were laughing.

He wasn't sure he would have been able to explain the moment to anyone had they asked. Yet there he was, laughing about being drenched with water during a heated make-out session. And that that make-out session had come after they'd both shared aspects of their lives neither of them had wanted to share before. He was beginning to understand why she'd pushed him away the night before, though why she'd walked away that afternoon was still a mystery. But he was making progress. And that was enough for him.

For now.

'Didn't you check when high tide would be?' she asked, squeezing the water out her curls.

'Yes,' he replied indignantly. 'And that *wasn't* high tide.' His eyes lifted to see storm clouds coming their way. 'I think we're in for one of the island's surprise summer storms,' he said and grabbed her hand just as thunder boomed.

'Shouldn't we clear the—'

She broke off when she looked back, and saw that there was nothing to clear from the rock they'd been on. The ocean had claimed the table and food, and a flash of lightning joined the ominous thunder.

'Come on. We should go before—'

With another boom above them, rain poured down, cutting his words off. Together they ran down the path they'd come from, the candles now extinguished, the rain coming down so hard that there was no smoke giving away that they'd once been lit.

Knowing how far the front of the castle was, Zacchaeus led Nalini down the side of the building, a route he hadn't used since he was a child. He saw their guards ahead of them now and realised—of course—that they would never really have any privacy. He thanked the heavens that he and Nalini had been stopped before they'd given their guards a more exciting show, and was grateful when he saw the door he'd been heading for open in front of them.

A few seconds later, they were inside the castle's kitchen.

It looked nothing like it had when he'd been a child. Though, as his eyes moved through the room, he realised that was largely because it was empty. The only people there were them and their two guards—one from Kirtida and one from Mattan—both of whom he dismissed to get into dry clothing.

'We should probably change into some dry clothes too,' she said, crossing her arms in front of her chest. It blocked his view of her breasts, though, considering the state of her clothing, that was probably for the best.

'Yes,' he replied. 'But we haven't eaten anything yet.'

'What? Oh, yes, of course.'

'You have to eat.'

'I do?'

'Especially because you didn't have dinner last night either.'

'Oh, it's fine. Besides, it's late,' she said, removing one arm quickly to gesture around them. 'There's a reason no one is here.'

'We are.'

'And now you're going to tell me that you have an amazing set of culinary skills?' she asked dryly.

'Actually, yes, I do.'

CHAPTER THIRTEEN

'YOU'RE KIDDING, RIGHT?' Nalini scoffed. 'There's no way you have the abilities it takes to work in a kitchen like this.'

He crossed his arms, drawing her eyes to the muscles she could see clearly through the wet shirt he wore. She swallowed.

'Would you like to make that bet with me, Your Royal Highness?'

'I would certainly like to make that bet with you,' she replied, but right at that moment a chill went through her. 'But does it have to be now? I'm freezing.'

'I can make a fire for us.'

'There's no fireplace in here.'

He smirked. 'Follow me.'

He led her through an archway on one side of the kitchen to the cosiest room she'd ever seen in her life. It was small, with just enough space to fit its two armchairs and a coffee table comfortably. There was a fireplace on the other side of the room—small, too, though she knew it would fill the room with heat. The windows gave her a view of the ocean thrashing against the shore, the raindrops partially obscuring it.

She felt her eyebrows lift. 'Are you trying to impress me?'

'Yes,' he replied, giving her that lazy smile again. Her stomach tumbled and a faint throb of panic began to pump through her veins. She ignored it and watched as he crouched down and in a few quick movements had a fire crackling.

'This room's been here for as long as I can remember. I think it must have been a pantry at some point long ago, but then became a place the kitchen staff could relax in. To me, it was always just the place I would come to when—' He broke off abruptly.

'When...?'

'When I needed company,' he said with a smile, but it held none of the ease of the one he'd given her before. 'The chef had a particular fondness for me.'

'Had?'

'Yes. He died a few years ago.'

'I'm sorry.'

'Thank you,' he replied softly. 'He was a good man. And he taught me how to cook. Prepared to eat your words? Literally?'

She laughed. 'Go ahead, impress me.'

He left the room and Nalini took the chance to survey the damage the ocean and rain had done. Her dress was clinging to her body, the material giving everyone who cared to look a free view of her underwear. She shivered, but knew it wasn't because of the cold. Rather, it was the reminder that *Zacchaeus* had cared to look. In fact, he'd done a lot more than look…

Warmth went through her and she kneeled in front of the fire, using it as an excuse for the increase in temperature. She didn't want to think about what had happened between them. About what had *nearly* happened. If she did, she would be giving into the panic she still felt in her blood. And in that moment she didn't want to panic. She didn't want to think about what she should or shouldn't have done.

So instead she focused on what had come before the kiss.

They'd shared things with one another. Had

teased. Flirted. The time she'd spent with Zacchaeus that evening had done a lot to bridge the distance between them. Distance she knew she had caused, too.

It had been a shock to learn that King Jaydon was ill. But the more she thought about it, the more she realised that it shouldn't have been so surprising. She'd heard the whispers, just as she'd told him. Xavier had mentioned it too, when he'd spoken about Zacchaeus. But both of them had brushed the possibility aside. It seemed too far-fetched that the reason for Zacchaeus's behaviour was something so simple. Too easy.

But, after listening to Zacchaeus, she knew it had been anything but easy.

Knowing that the coup wasn't something that he'd wanted had her seeing him in a different light. Or perhaps not, she considered, rubbing her hands together. She hadn't really wanted to believe that he was capable of overthrowing his father. She might have convinced herself that he was, but that was only because *he'd* wanted her to.

It made her wonder what had changed. Why had he decided to tell her the truth now? Why was he showing her that the ruthless, selfish man he'd claimed to be the night she'd arrived on Kirtida wasn't the real Zacchaeus? Did he know that what he'd told her showed her the opposite? That a man who would give up his reputation to make his sick father happy was actually selfless and kind?

'I've brought towels and blankets,' Zacchaeus said, walking back into the room. He'd changed, she saw, and frowned. Even though the long-sleeved top he'd paired with jeans made him look more casual and just as hunky as ever.

'That's not fair.'

'That I brought you towels?'

'That you changed.' She took a towel from him and gestured for him to put the rest on the seat next to him.

'I agree. But the guards brought down these dry clothes and what was I supposed to say? No, thank you?'

'Yes,' she told him. 'Because if you're forcing me to stay wet and miserable down here, the very least you could do is be wet and miserable with me.'

He gave a long-suffering sigh. 'You're right. Which is why I also brought you this.'

He took out a T-shirt and sweatpants from between the top two towels, and she felt a smile creep onto her lips.

'Why couldn't you lead with that?' she asked, taking the clothes from him.

'Because you scrunch your nose up when you're annoyed, and I really like it.'

As though proving his point, he pressed a soft kiss on her nose and left the room again before she could process it. Somewhere in her mind, a voice was shouting at her for the way his action made her feel, but it was so foggy and vague that she ignored it.

She dried off and changed quickly, and realised the clothes she was now drowning in were his. It had her frowning when he came in again, this time with two steaming mugs.

'Are these yours?' she asked, watching him set the drinks on the table.

His eyes ran over her. 'Yes. The guards didn't want to search in your things, so they took whatever they could find from my room. You don't like them?'

'No, no, they're fine,' she said hurriedly, and gave her hair one last pat with the towel before curling in the armchair, throwing a blanket over her and picking up her drink. She moaned as she took the first sip of hot chocolate, and then blushed when she saw the look in Zacchaeus's eyes.

'What brand is this?' she asked, trying to avoid a repeat performance of their make-out session. Even though her body was urging her to do just that. 'I've never tasted anything like this before. It's delicious.'

'You wouldn't have,' he replied. 'I made it from scratch.'

'You're lying.'

'Nope.' He grinned, and she thought he'd never seemed less like a king. 'I told you I had skills.'

'Remind me never to doubt you again.'

Something passed between them after she'd said the words, and it stayed with her even after he'd left to finish making their meal. It was as if she'd been pledging her loyalty to him, she thought. And realised that, essentially, she was doing just that.

Because, despite the fact that she now knew

Zacchaeus hadn't wanted to overthrow his father, she had no intention of telling her brother or Leyna. Even though it might help the negotiations for Mattan. Even though it might mean that she wouldn't have to marry him.

The thought sent a shiver down her spine and her fingers tightened around the mug she held with both hands. What was happening to her? Did she *want* to marry Zacchaeus now? All of a sudden? When the hell had that happened?The thought made the panic harder to ignore, and when he returned with two plates she had to fight to keep herself from acting differently than she had before.

'This looks delicious,' she said, taking the plate and fork from him.

'All I could do on short notice, I'm afraid.'

She nodded and dug into the creamy pasta dish. One part of her brain told her it *was* delicious, while the other kept bringing up the thoughts she was trying very hard to ignore.

'What's wrong?' he asked her, and she looked over at him in surprise. His plate was empty, as was hers, and she realised that they'd eaten the entire meal in silence.

'Nothing,' she told him, setting the plate down next to his on the coffee table. 'It was really wonderful.'

'What's wrong, Nalini?' he asked again, his voice soft but urgent, and she found herself answering him before she fully knew that she was.

'Why didn't you come to the State Banquet?'

He'd been waiting for the question since he'd told her the truth about the coup, and yet somehow, he still felt unprepared for it. Again, he wondered whether he should tell her. His heart told him to—and that frightened him more than the voice inside his head telling him not to.

But he'd been led by his head for so long. He wanted to follow his heart for just one night. This night.

He took a breath, felt the tension of what he was about to say stiffen his muscles. 'I wanted to. I was going to. But my father...' He trailed off, leaned forward, but didn't look at her. 'He had a bad night that night, and I needed to stay with him.' Now he did look at her. 'It wasn't a choice.'

'And after? Why didn't you call us? Why did you refuse to see Xavier and Leyna?'

He opened his mouth but no words came out. Tried again, but the same thing happened. It was harder than he'd thought it would be, he realised, rubbing a hand over his face. He'd never spoken about his mother before. He'd never told anyone about her infidelity. Of course, he was sure the staff knew. His mother had gone on way too many 'diplomatic trips' for it to be a secret.

But *he'd* never told anyone before. And though he wanted to tell Nalini and continue building the trust between them, it just wasn't that easy.

'Let me guess,' she said softly. 'It's complicated.'

'It is,' he replied gratefully, but saw the hurt in her eyes. 'I'm not just saying that, Nalini. The situation I'm in—the one *we're* in—*is* complicated.'

Silence followed his words. He sighed. 'Why is it so important for you to know?'

'Because it's the reason I'm here.' Her voice was still soft, but there was fire in her eyes. 'If you'd come to the Banquet, none of it would have got to this point. Xavier and Leyna wouldn't have got engaged, and neither would we.'

'So that's it.' Disappointment sharpened his words. 'You're asking me because you're still angry about me forcing this marriage.'

'No, that's not it.' She ran her fingers through the front of her hair, and when they couldn't go any further shook out the curls. 'I'm not angry any more. I actually don't think that I ever was angry at you. I understood your political position. I looked at Xavier and Leyna, and knew that both of them would have done the same. *Had*, even.'

She paused and did the same thing with her hair, but from a different angle. 'I came here for political reasons. But those aren't the only reasons I'm staying.' Her hand fell down to her lap and clutched the blanket over her legs. 'You can trust me, Zacchaeus. I want you to trust me.'

She hadn't told him how that related to the other reasons she was staying. But he could connect the dots for himself. There was something…more happening between them. And, because of it, she was asking him to trust her.

He could ask her for the same. And he would, he thought. But, right now, the uncertainty in her eyes told him that she needed him to take the first step.

'My mother isn't on Kirtida.' He said the words in a rush, and braced himself to tell her the rest. 'She left over two months ago, right before I took over the Crown.'

'Why?'

'Because she's been having an affair with the vice-president of Macoa.'

Stunned silence greeted his words, and then she stammered, 'I… I'm not sure what to say.'

'You don't have to say anything. It is what it is.'

'What it is…is terrible. I'm so sorry.'

He nodded, accepted her apology. And waited for her to realise what his words meant. He didn't have to wait very long.

'Wait—Macoa? Is that why—?'

'Yes.' But because it didn't make sense without her having the full story, he took a deep breath and told her. 'The affair started long ago. I don't know exactly when, but I remember hearing my parents fight once. My mother told my father she'd given him an heir—why did he still care about what she did with whom? So I know it started long ago.'

'When did you find out?'

'On my eighth birthday. It hadn't been the first fight I'd witnessed between them, and it wasn't the last. But it was the first time I'd heard about the affair.'

'On your birthday,' she murmured. 'That's terrible.'

He shrugged. 'It didn't really matter. I was never under the illusion that my parents had the best marriage. I'd understood long before then that there was a difference in the way my parents acted when they were around people and when they were alone—or with me.' He paused. 'It didn't affect me too much.'

'I don't think that's true,' she said softly.

'Maybe not,' he allowed, but shrugged again. 'I survived it.'

She nodded. 'What did this have to do with the Banquet?'

'We got word that night that my mother wanted a divorce.' He exhaled unsteadily. 'They were demanding it, and threatened us with economic sanctions if we didn't agree. There was even a threat of more.'

'That's *terrible*. How did the vice-president manage to make his personal business political?'

'He has more power than the president, and the man knows it. The only reason he's still vice-president is because he wants my mother by his side before he moves up.'

'That's what he told you?'

'He didn't have to. When I heard that she'd left, I spent weeks thinking about it. I'm not one hundred per cent sure, and I might be wrong, but I think he wants to be in power with her. To form some kind of political power couple. I don't know,' he said, shaking his head.

It had seemed so logical in his mind, but now it sounded foolish. Unless he faced the unwelcome fact that his mother and Francisco were genuinely in love and wanted to rule together. But that made his mother sound more human—more sensitive—than she was.

'And then you told your father about it,' she said, realisation dawning on her face.

'No, she contacted my father directly and told him. The shock worsened his already weak heart, and I couldn't attend the Banquet.'

'Why didn't you just come to us and tell us the truth? We would have understood.'

'That we'd made up a coup so that my father didn't seem weak in front of his estranged wife and her lover?' he scoffed. 'You really think they would have understood that?' He shook his head. 'No one knows about my father's illness—not definitively, at least—except the two of us.'

'Not even your mother?' He shook his head. 'How did she not suspect?'

'She didn't care,' he said bitterly, and then told himself to rein it in. 'But she'd left before his symptoms became visible.'

'So you couldn't tell us anything.' She frowned. 'But you knew you had to tell us something eventually.'

'Yes. Which was exactly what I had to figure out in the month that I refused to see them. To talk to them.' His fingers itched for something to do so he didn't have to feel so damn helpless. 'I was lost and I didn't have anyone to talk to. I couldn't talk to my father in the state he was—still is—in. I had to figure it all out on my own.'

'And Xavier and Leyna's marriage gave you the push you needed.'

'I knew I had to ask them to consider adjusting the Protection clause. I was afraid the sanctions would only be the beginning. I still am.'

A long pause followed his words, and he watched as she played with her fingers in her lap. He had no idea what she was thinking. Had no idea whether she'd be on the phone to her brother as soon as they parted ways to tell him the truth.

'Is that why you brought out your fleet? To protect your kingdom?'

'Yes.'

'So you never intended to use it against Mattan and Aidara.'

'No.'

She nodded and bit her lip, turning it white. 'And everything has felt so rushed, so urgent, because you want to make sure your kingdom is protected?'

'And the Isles,' he added. 'My people first,

yes, always, but I never wanted to jeopardise the alliance between our kingdoms. When I heard about the economic sanctions I knew it would affect Mattan and Aidara, too. And then I heard about Leyna and Xavier's engagement and I realised that we needed to be strengthened in the same way.'

He paused. 'I'm not saying I didn't take advantage of the situation to get what my kingdom needed, but I want the Alliance of the Three Isles intact. I want us to be just as strong together as we were when my father ruled. And that meant marriage to you. I'm… I'm sorry that you were collateral damage in that.'

Her eyes told him that she accepted his apology, and he felt relief spread through him. And then she said, 'You don't know when you'll get another threat from Macoa, do you?'

'No. But it could be any time.'

'And you won't ask your father to give your mother a divorce.'

He clenched his jaw. 'I can't, Nalini. If I did, I'd be responsible for killing him.'

'You think she won't go to him again? Directly?'

'I've made sure that won't happen.'

There was a long pause before she spoke again.

'It sounds like you need to speed up the negotiations, Zac,' she said softly. 'Because we're setting a date for our wedding. For next week.'

CHAPTER FOURTEEN

NALINI COULDN'T QUITE believe that she'd made the offer.

She wasn't sure if it was the look on his face or the way he'd trusted her. Or the fact that he'd just confirmed to her that he was a good man— and that he didn't see himself that way.

Perhaps it was because no matter how much she wanted to offer him the same courtesy—to completely trust him with her own secrets—she couldn't bring herself to say them out loud.

'Excuse me?' he said, disbelief clear in his tone.

'You heard me,' she replied mildly, despite the way her chest tightened. 'We'll get married next week.'

'But…how? *Why?*'

'We'll manage it. And because…' She faltered. 'Because it'll help you. Won't it?'

'Yes, but I don't expect you to do this for me.'

His eyes were solemn, his voice sincere, and she felt her heart palpitate.

'Fine then, I'm not doing it for you.'

'Liar.'

She lifted her shoulders. 'It's happening, Zac, so you can—'

She was cut off when his lips touched hers—a fast, fierce kiss that told her exactly what her offer had meant to him. Her throat closed when they parted—when she saw the emotion in his eyes—but she smiled.

'I don't expect you to do this at all.'

'I know.'

He nodded and when the emotion whirled inside her she realised it was time to leave.

'We can meet tomorrow to start discussing things, okay?' She uncurled her feet from under her and set them to the ground.

'Sure.'

When she looked at him she saw that his thoughts had distracted him, and she murmured, 'Goodnight,' before she walked back to her room.

She took her shower quickly, and vigorously rubbed her body dry when she got out. As though it would help her to no longer feel as dirty—as guilty—as she did. He hadn't asked her for the details of it—about what she was keeping from him, though she knew he wanted to know. Though she was sure that he'd stopped himself from asking her what that *thing* was that she'd spoken to him about.

And the fact that he'd told her about his father, his mother… Her heart ached just thinking about it. About what that poor little boy had gone through. No wonder he hid his emotions. No wonder he didn't want to open himself up. He'd been hurt—terribly—by the people who were supposed to love him most. His mother through her infidelity and his father by forcing him to become someone he was not.

But now she had to face the fact that perhaps he'd told her about his troubles because he wanted the same honesty from her. And she wanted to tell him, but the story in no way compared to his. It was stupid, she thought now. Petty even. And had nothing to do with whether or not she could trust her gut with him now.

No, a boy who had broken her heart didn't come close to what he'd been through. It was trivial, she thought again, and ignored the inner voice that told her there was so much more to what had happened to her that night on the beach than just her heart being broken.

It didn't matter, she told herself. She would commit to planning their wedding and take some of the pressure off Zacchaeus. He had enough to worry about.

Her plan might not come close to opening up to him, but it was all that she could give him.

She hoped it would be enough.

Zacchaeus wasn't entirely sure how to feel about the current state of things between him and his future wife.

They were knee-deep into planning their wedding—three days in, four more to go—and she'd been avoiding him. Not physically—they saw each other often, more so since he and Leyna and Xavier had finalised their negotiations.

But the day after she'd told him they would move their wedding up, she'd gone with him to Mattan to tell her family. And whatever that discussion had entailed had her pulling away from him.

Whenever he broached the topic she would make up something about the wedding to talk to him about. She hadn't mentioned anything he'd told her that night again and, since nothing had changed in his negotiations with Leyna and Xavier, she obviously hadn't told her brother about it either.

It had quietened the voice that told him he'd been a fool to tell her about his parents. And now that it was quiet he could feel the relief flooding through him that he'd finally told someone. And not just anyone—Nalini. She had a way about her that made him feel as though he could tell her anything. Finally sharing the secret he'd been carrying alone for years had made him feel free, as if he were no longer pushing against an invisible force whenever he wanted to move forward.

It killed him that the person who'd finally freed him from that was now pulling away from him.

'White or purple?' she asked as he walked into the room that had become the wedding headquarters. He narrowed his eyes at the concoction—it was the only word he could come up with—of flowers she was standing in front of, and tried to figure out what she wanted him to say.

'White?'

She gave a satisfied nod. 'I thought so, too.'

'Then why did you ask?'

'It never hurts to have a second opinion.'

He would have smirked if he hadn't noticed that she immediately walked away from him, putting the table with the flowers between them. When she didn't look up at him again, he felt his jaw clench before he made a split-second decision.

'Out,' he roared, and felt surprise ripple through the people in the room. He knew he would have to do damage control after, since he was acting in exactly the way they expected him to, but told himself it was worth it. He couldn't take another day of this Nalini.

And he sure as hell didn't want to marry this Nalini.

He shook his head at her when she moved around the table as well—as though she were going to leave, too—and waited until they were alone before he spoke.

'What did they tell you?'

'Who?' she replied in a bewildered voice.

'Your mother and grandmother. What did they say when you told them we were moving the wedding up?'

The colour drained from her cheeks, but she straightened her shoulders. 'Nothing worth repeating.'

'But clearly it was important to you because you've been treating me differently since the moment you left that room with them.'

'I have *not*.'

'Yes, you have,' he growled, and felt his fingers curl into a fist. 'It's like that day at the beach never happened. And since we both know that it did—' he gestured around them at the proof of it '—the very least you can do is tell me why.'

'Nothing's changed, Zacchaeus.'

'So the fact that you're calling me that doesn't mean anything then?'

'That's what I've called you all my life,' she said impatiently. 'I'm going to need time to get used to calling you something else. So, since I'm telling you now that I haven't been pulling away from you, can we call back everyone who's been helping us plan this wedding?'

He didn't answer, and waited as the silence stretched. Waited in the hope that she would give him the honesty he'd given her. Or at least tell him why she couldn't.

'Is this really how you want things to be between us?' he asked her quietly when waiting didn't help.

'Things are fine—'

'No, they're not,' he snapped. 'Do you remember what you told me once, when you first got here? That I wouldn't be alone—that I didn't have to be—if I confided in you? And now that I have, you're telling me that you're not interested in giving me the same courtesy?'

A long silence followed his words, and then he shook his head and turned to walk out.

'I don't know how to confide in you,' she called after him. 'I don't know how to tell you this…this *thing*. It's so small compared to what you went through. How am I supposed to tell you about it when it's so insignificant?'

'But clearly it's not,' he told her, turning back. He wanted to walk to her side—to take her hands in his and squeeze, comfort. But his feet were cemented to the ground and he couldn't find the willpower to move them. 'Whatever you've gone through has affected you so much that you can't tell me about it. Just based on that, it's significant.'

She bit her lip, and then sighed. 'They weren't happy. My grandmother and mother, I mean.'

Though it wasn't what he wanted from her, it was a start. 'I didn't imagine they would be.'

'It's what's best for the kingdom.' Her eyes changed with the words, and he knew it was because that wasn't the only reason. 'And the funny thing is that I think they would have agreed to it if it had been their idea.'

'So they're not unhappy about you marrying me, just that you're marrying…against their wishes?'

'Basically.'

'Surely that's not true.'

'Unfortunately, it is.' She brushed away a curl that had escaped the tie on the top of her head. 'When you live your entire life that way it becomes more believable.'

'And it's why you can't tell me about that *thing*, isn't it?'

'Probably.'

He nodded, and tried to figure out his feelings about it. Could he feel betrayed that she didn't want to tell him? He wasn't sure if he *could*, but he certainly felt that way. Because he hadn't had anyone to trust growing up either. Not about the real stuff, anyway.

His father had been an excellent guide on becoming King. He'd been patient and open about what he'd learnt. But when it came to Michelle, he was the complete opposite. Zacchaeus would never be able to talk to him about how much his mother's disinterest had hurt. He would never be able to ask his father why Michelle had hurt him in that way, or why she'd chosen a random man over her family. The only time Jaydon had truly spoken about what his wife had done was after she'd already left.

And that was because of what she'd left behind.

'It's not easy for me to talk to you either, you know,' he heard himself say. 'But I did. Because I thought that… Well, I didn't want to be alone. But I guess that, despite that, I still am.'

His hurt—his anger—had him walking out of the room without waiting for a reply.

CHAPTER FIFTEEN

'YOU SHOULDN'T HAVE to do this,' Alika said in that sweet way she had. Except today that sweetness was tinged with anger and indignation.

'It doesn't matter,' Nalini said, and smoothed down the front of her dress. 'I *am* doing this. Though I'll admit, it isn't happening the way I'd imagined.'

'Of course not. You should be getting married in your own kingdom to a man you chose for yourself.'

Nalini whirled around. 'You didn't choose your husband for yourself. How is this any different?'

'Oh, you know what I mean,' she said, and waved a hand.

Nalini narrowed her eyes as she watched her sister busy herself with her make-up. She *wasn't* sure what Alika meant. All she knew was that her sister looked more tired than Nalini had ever seen her. And it worried her.

206 FALLING FOR HIS CONVENIENT QUEEN

Not only for Alika's sake, but for her own too. Because it was Alika's unhappiness that made her look that way. As if she'd given up hope. And if *Alika* had given up hope, what hope did *Nalini* have?

Especially now that she'd alienated Zacchaeus, who would be her partner after they married.

Not for the first time since that night she'd offered to move their wedding up, she wondered whether she'd made a terrible mistake. Whether she'd let her sympathy after hearing about Zacchaeus's life, about his parents, about what it all must have meant for him growing up, sway her into marrying him when she should have waited. When she should have used what he'd told her as leverage to release her from this marriage.

But then she'd meant it when she'd said that she'd forgiven him for forcing their marriage. She *did* understand his political decision—and, now that she knew the facts, didn't blame him for acting the way he had. But now she knew that she'd hurt him. She knew that pushing him away, not telling him about Josh, had hurt him. And, despite how much that fact hurt *her*, she couldn't bring herself to do anything about it.

And now here they were. On the day they were going to be married. The Protection clause had been finalised, and Zacchaeus had signed the papers reaffirming the alliance that morning. It had been a sign of faith on his side, she knew. He'd been repaying her for keeping what she knew to herself.

Even though he was still angry with her.

A knock on the door kept her from thinking about it again, though it sent an entirely different uneasiness through her stomach. She thought of the night before—of welcoming her family to Kirtida for the rehearsal dinner. And thanked the heavens—again—that they'd opened the dinner to all guests who had arrived at that stage.

If they hadn't, it would have been much *more* awkward than it already was. Zacchaeus's family's absence was the elephant in the room, one they'd blamed on the coup. But the truth was that anyone who saw Zacchaeus's father would know the man was gravely ill. Nalini could confirm that, considering she'd finally been able to meet with him. She'd hidden her shock and had spoken to the man as she would at any other time. Zacchaeus had thanked her for it and, for the first time then, she'd seen the effect his father's illness was having on him.

And then, of course, there was his mother. Who would *definitely* not be attending.

Though there were times that evening that she'd envied Zacchaeus. Her own mother and grandmother had barely looked at her, and hadn't said a word to Zacchaeus. Leyna, Xavier, Alika and her husband, Spencer, had all made an effort, but things were still tense. Xavier was still angry. Alika was sad. And Nalini had felt responsible for it all, unfairly, she knew, and had busied herself by focusing on all her other guests.

It meant her wedding wouldn't be as wonderful as she'd imagined once upon a time. But what did that matter? Hadn't she given up on a fairy tale wedding years ago? Hadn't she given up on the hope, the romance, she'd wanted it to have?

She shut her eyes against the thought that Zacchaeus had woken all those dreams in her again, and forced herself to be in the present. Though she knew it was that thought that had her keeping things strictly work-related between them.

She blew out a breath as she made it from

the little cottage on the church's property to the church. Her heart thudded at the prospect of what was about to happen, but slowed when she saw Xavier waiting for her outside.

'There's still time to pull out,' Xavier said as soon as he saw her, much like he had the day she'd decided to marry Zacchaeus. And, just like she had then, she refused.

'I'm not pulling out, Xavier.' But she brushed a kiss on his cheek. 'I know what I'm doing.'

'Do you, though?' he asked, his eyes serious. 'I've seen the way he looks at you. And the way you look at him,' he added when she opened her mouth to protest.

'Oh, that's… I mean, that's nothing. There's nothing,' she said more firmly. 'We've just become friends.'

'With that tension between the two of you?' he replied with raised eyebrows.

'Let's just get on with it, shall we?' she told him, determined not to get cold feet.

'If that's what you want?' he asked one more time, and when she nodded he took her arm and slid it through his. 'You look beautiful, by the way.'

Love warmed her chest. 'And you couldn't start out by saying that?'

'No. That would contravene the brother code. I'm violating it as we speak.'

She laughed and squeezed his arm, thanking him silently for distracting her. And then she squared her shoulders and prepared herself to get married.

The music started playing, and Nalini watched as Alika walked through the church doors as her only bridesmaid. Her heart sped up again, but it didn't keep her from noticing that the hard work she'd put into the details of her wedding had paid off.

A floral arch made entirely of different kinds of white flowers framed the door to the church. She let Xavier lead them as she walked through it, and instead looked at how perfectly they matched the all-white décor in the church.

And kept her eyes on the flowers on either side of the altar instead of the back of the man she was walking down the aisle towards.

But then she remembered she was supposed to look like an excited bride, and put a nervous smile on her face. Not that she had to pretend much about the nerves. Even though their wedding was small compared to other royal weddings—with only guests who could make the short notice present—she still felt anxious. As though each one of them could see straight through her. Through them.

All the while she was studiously avoiding her mother and grandmother's gazes.

She and Xavier reached the front of the church then, and Zacchaeus turned towards her. Her breath caught at the sight of him in his uniform. She'd seen him wearing it countless times before, but somehow, now, her mind decided to notice every aspect of him. Probably because it knew how much she was trying to fight her attraction to him.

So, of course, she suddenly saw how his military jacket fitted him as if it had been designed with his broad shoulders in mind. How those intimidatingly sexy lines of his face seemed to match the tone of the uniform exactly. Serious, powerful, *demanding*. And now all of that was hers—the unwanted thought popped into her mind and she forced it away.

But then came the emotion. She wondered if

her own was as clear on her face as what she saw on his now. It had her heart beating even harder, but Zacchaeus gripped her hand tightly as Xavier handed her over, and just before they turned to the priest he whispered, 'I don't think I've seen any woman look more beautiful than you do right now.'

The words made her flush, and she squeezed his hand. Then she pulled back her shoulders and faced the priest, focusing on getting through the ceremony.

She didn't quite feel as if it was happening to her. No, she felt as if she'd floated up above herself and was watching two people who were marrying for convenience say vows that she'd once thought should mean something. It was only when the priest announced that Zacchaeus could kiss his bride that she fell back into herself. Except it didn't feel like falling—more as if a vortex was sucking her back into her body.

She held her breath as she faced him, and then felt the air leave her lungs when she saw the emotion on his face. She didn't deserve the compassion, the tenderness she saw there. She'd pulled away from him because she'd realised that night they'd spent on the beach had gone too far. They'd gone too far. And that that night had somehow taken the place of the last time she'd been on a beach with a man. That now the beach was a beautiful place for her again, and not a reminder of the mistakes that she'd made.

Except she feared that it was. As she looked into Zacchaeus's eyes—as she felt herself anticipate his kiss—she knew that something had changed between them. She knew that the fact that she'd offered to marry him sooner to protect his kingdom—to give him peace of mind—had come from that. And because he'd somehow eased the pain of what had happened with Josh, that change had been extreme.

She was so scared of it that she'd refused to speak to him other than about the wedding. He'd told her his deepest secrets and that was how she'd responded. It was terrible. But what choice did she have? She was falling—fast—and she didn't know whether she was prepared to hit the ground.

So she didn't know why he was looking at her like that now. Or why he'd lowered his head and kissed her softly, his arms going around her re-

FALLING FOR HIS CONVENIENT QUEEN

assuringly, as though he would always comfort and support her.

Or why she'd kissed him back, and felt her arms do the same.

And then the kiss was over and she went back to watching it all happen outside her body.

She wasn't quite sure how she got through it all. But, before she knew it, she was sharing her first dance with her husband.

Husband.

'You did an amazing job at planning this in such a short time,' Zacchaeus said softly.

'*We* did,' she corrected, her eyes moving over the flowers, the draping, the fairy lights that created quite the scene. Almost like the wedding she'd pictured before she'd convinced herself it was all pointless.

'I'm not entirely sure if that's true, but I'll take it.' He twirled her around and then drew her in closer than the dance required. 'You're unhappy.'

'What? No, I'm not.'

'You mean it doesn't bother you that your grandmother and mother glower at us at every opportunity they get?'

She winced as her gaze swept over the two

women, who were doing just that. 'There's nothing I can do about it.'

'But you want to.'

'I suppose. Even though I know it's pointless.' She thought back to that day on the beach, and how terribly they'd treated her when she'd come back. And now, how poorly they were treating her even though she knew she'd done the right thing. 'But I'm learning to get over it.'

'And this all started because of that…that *thing* that happened when you were younger?'

His eyes missed nothing, she thought. 'Yes.'

'But you won't tell me about it because you've decided it's easier that way.'

She kept the space between her eyebrows smooth, though it desperately wanted to crease. 'I'm not sure what you mean.'

'It's done now, Nalini. We're married. What are you going to use as an excuse to pull away from me now?'

The music ended and after they bowed, he walked out of the hall without another look at her. For a moment she stood there, stunned that her new husband had just walked out on her, and then Xavier was there, taking Zacchaeus's place.

It took her a few seconds to realise what had happened, and then she cleared her throat. 'Thanks.'

'You're welcome.'

'Just say it.'

'What?' he asked innocently.

'I know you have something to say. When have you ever not? So, say it.'

He made a non-committal sound deep in his throat, and they danced for a minute before either of them spoke again.

'Come on, Xav,' Nalini said impatiently now.

'What do you think I want to say, Lini?'

'Aren't you going to ask me about why Zacchaeus left?'

'Why did he?'

'I don't know.' But she did, and when he didn't answer her she sighed. 'I upset him.'

'Why?' Now *she* didn't answer *him*. Because what could she say? That she'd hurt him by pulling away from him after he'd trusted her? That when he'd asked her to do the same she'd refused?

It had strained things between them worse than ever before. Worse because now they were hurting each other. Because feelings and trust meant they had more power over each other. And because she knew that she sighed again.

'I need to speak to him.'

Xavier nodded. 'Fine. After the song.' And when the song finished he brushed a kiss on her forehead and looked down earnestly into her face. 'Be careful.'

She smiled. 'Is that your way of giving me your approval?'

'You're married to him now, Lini. There's not much I can do about it.' His tone was serious, but then a light glinted in his eye. 'Besides, Leyna told me to butt out. So…' He shrugged and then grinned at her, and she couldn't help but laugh.

'I think I'm going to like having her as a sister.'

'I think so too.'

She nodded and threw her arms around him. Squeezed. 'I love you.'

'You too. And I'm proud of you.' When she drew back she saw that his eyes shone with sincerity. 'I know I didn't support you about this at first, and that was wrong of me. Because I can see that you've grown, and changed. You're going to be okay, Lini. I know it.'

Her throat thick with emotion from the words she'd longed to hear, Nalini kissed his cheek and went to find her husband.

CHAPTER SIXTEEN

ZACCHAEUS FELT AS IF he were carrying a rock on his shoulders. That was how bad the tension was between him and his new wife.

He closed his eyes at the term—at the emotion the term brought.

Because his *wife* was the reason he felt so damn raw. How did she manage to make him *feel* so much when he was so mad at her? How had the moment he'd seen her in that wedding dress crept so deeply into his heart? And why had he wanted to show her, the moment they'd kissed, that he wouldn't take their vows for granted—that he didn't want her to either?

It didn't bode well for his future. And it had turned him into the surly man everyone already thought that he was. Except now he had no hope of changing their minds when he'd be facing the reason for his mood every day for the rest of his life.

'I don't suppose I should be worried that my husband's run away from me on our wedding day?' a voice said from behind him, but he didn't turn when he answered.

'The wedding was just a farce,' he said in a steely voice. 'It shouldn't matter what your husband has or hasn't done, considering that he's only a husband in name.'

'But that's not true, is it?'

He felt her move in next to him, though she stared out of the window of the tower room just as he did. Just then he realised why he'd been drawn to that room out of all in the castle. Not only had it given him the privacy he'd craved, but it also reminded him of her. Of how, for the first time, he'd seen himself through her eyes. Of how, for the first time, he'd seen himself as something other than the man—than the king— he thought he was.

He also finally understood why his ancestor had jumped from the window.

Zacchaeus didn't know what else *he* could do to show Nalini she could trust him. That she could confide in him. Did he need to jump, too?

Why did he suddenly feel so desperate that that option seemed viable?

'You know there's more between us than a farce.'

'Really?' he asked mildly, ignoring the effect her words had on his heart. 'Because I was under the impression that you were happy with the way things are between us.'

'I'm not.' She walked to the front of him, forcing him to look at her. And, damn it, it was as if she knew exactly what seeing her in that flowing white dress, her curls spiralling around her face underneath her crown, would do to him. 'I've hurt you. How can I be happy about that?'

'You seem happy with it,' he replied in a biting voice. 'You seem fine with keeping me at a distance.'

'Well, I'm not. But, like I told you before, I don't know how to tell you this.'

'If we're going to repeat this—'

'It happened when I was too young to know about the reality of the world,' she interrupted him. 'Of *our* world. And now it feels foolish. *I* feel foolish, and I don't want you to see me that way.'

He didn't move—couldn't. Afraid that if he

did, he would break whatever was happening between them.

'When I came here, I realised it was an opportunity for me to start over.' She turned her back to him now, and stepped aside to give him back his view of the sea. 'You didn't know about *that day*—' she said those words bitterly '—and you couldn't judge me for it. You wouldn't think of me as careless. So I didn't want to tell you, and I still don't.' There was a pause. 'But if you need to know, Zacchaeus, then just say the word and I'll tell you.'

'That's not fair,' he said in a low voice. 'If I tell you I want to know, you'll hold it against me for the rest of our marriage.'

'I won't.'

'Really? Because I've seen resentment in a marriage. I've seen one spouse blame another for things that couldn't possibly be their fault. So forgive me if I don't believe you.'

'Maybe I just need to hear you ask,' she said softly.

'Maybe I just need to hear you tell me even though I didn't ask you to. Like when I told you about my parents.' He was angry now, and he knew it came from hurt. From doubt about whether he should have just kept things to himself. About whether telling her had been a terrible mistake. 'You're asking me to trust you, Nalini, and you haven't given me a reason to.'

'I haven't—' she said in disbelief. 'I haven't given you a reason to *trust me*? What about this wedding?' She gestured between them. 'What about the fact that I didn't tell my brother or Leyna about the real reason you needed the alliance's protection? That I put your kingdom ahead of my own so that you could have peace of mind?' Her chest heaved beneath the lace detail of her dress. 'I might not be able to tell you about the day I was lured to the beach by a man I thought loved me, only to be made a fool of, but I did do all the rest. For you. For you to trust me. If that's not enough…'

She shook her head and then he saw the colour fade from her cheeks as she realised what she'd said.

'He hurt you?'

The anger he'd felt earlier was nothing compared to the heat that burned in his veins now.

'No.' She closed her eyes. 'Not in the way you mean.'

He couldn't resist now, and slid an arm around her waist. 'Tell me.'

Her muscles stiffened under his arm, and then he felt them relax. She was doing so deliberately, he realised, and marvelled at her strength.

'I was in love with him,' she started in a whisper. 'The hopeless, stupid kind that can only be felt by a teenager.' She paused. 'I met him at a festival in the castle. He was normal, and didn't have anything to do with high society or royalty. He was such a breath of fresh air.'

She sucked in a breath now and moved out of his embrace to lean her hands against the window pane. 'I told you I'd always been a little rebellious. The undutiful child. I hadn't got myself into any trouble to earn those labels, but my mother didn't need that. I just wasn't as amenable as my brother and sister, and listening to my mother's every word, every desire, for me was so *boring*. So if she told me to run along to my piano lesson, I'd detour to the library first. Or if I had etiquette training, I'd sneak away to practise the piano before. Or to paint,' she said with a smile over her shoulder for him. But it had already faded by the time she faced back to the window.

'Anyway, I met this boy—Josh—and I was so taken by how kind and free and *handsome* he was that I found ways to get him back to the castle. We'd only known each other for a month, but I was convinced that I would marry him. No,' she corrected herself, 'I was convinced that *he* would marry me. He told me he would, promised me that we'd spend our lives together. And then he'd kiss me so softly and sweetly, so what choice did I have but to believe him?'

'But he lied.'

She clenched her jaw. 'He lied. But not before he'd managed to get me to agree to sneak out of the castle with him. I'd refused before, knowing it would be unsafe. But he told me that he wanted to make our relationship more official, and somehow I got it into my mind that he was going to propose.' She gave a harsh bark of laughter. 'How stupid was that? I was seventeen years old and I thought a boy was going to propose to me. I thought I'd actually be able to marry him. A boy I'd met at a festival who had no part in high society or royalty.'

She shook her head again. 'Saying it aloud makes me sound even more stupid than I was.'

'Which was why you didn't want to tell me about it.'

'Yes. And I'm not even done yet.'

She walked away from the window and began pacing the floor. He was helpless to stop her and only watched as she did this to herself. Soon, he told himself. As soon as she was done, as soon as she'd got it all out, he would comfort her. And tell her that nothing she told him made him think of her as a fool.

'So I dressed up. I put on my finest jewels, my prettiest dress. I told myself that this would be the first night of the rest of our lives together. I would finally get the independence, the freedom, I'd always longed for. I'd ignored my grandmother's warnings about Josh—she'd realised what was happening when I began to find more and more reasons for him to come to the castle—and she'd told me that it would never last. That it would never last *and* that he didn't really want me.'

She laughed again, but this time it sounded horribly strangled. 'But I'd trained myself to ignore them. My mother and grandmother were so critical about everything and by then I already knew they saw me as the difficult one. As the problem child,' she added, and gave him a smile that reminded him of his words the first night she'd come to Kirtida. He understood now why she'd reacted the way she had.

'They just didn't want me to be happy, I told myself and snuck out of the castle to meet Josh where he told me to. It was on the beach,' she told him, and stopped pacing. Faced him. 'It was a lovely evening, and he was being as sweet as he always was. And I thought I was on an adventure. It was thrilling and so romantic. Until we started walking down the beach and I saw a group of teenagers around a fire.' She took another shaky breath. 'He assured me that he didn't know them, and that they wouldn't recognise us, but they were both lies. And when we reached them…' She faltered, and he watched as she drew herself up even taller. 'When we got there he left me and watched as the group tore at my clothing and jewels.'

'Nalini,' he whispered, horrified. She didn't back away when he moved forward, gripped her hands. They were like ice in his.

'He laughed at me,' she replied dully. 'They all did. And I could see in his eyes that he'd done all of it because he wanted to impress his friends. Never because he wanted to impress me. Or because he liked me even.'

'*He* was the idiot, not you,' he told her, and pressed a kiss to her forehead.

'He wasn't the one who thought they were in love with someone after a month.' She tried to rustle up a smile, but all he saw was a painful attempt to make something that had hurt her seem like it hadn't.

'What happened?'

'The castle guards found me. Alika had realised I was missing and had told Xavier, who sent the guards out for me.'

'They saved you.'

'Yes.'

'Were you hurt?'

'Bruises, scratches.' She lifted her shoulders and pulled her hands gently from his. 'I think they might have done more—' the words were said in a shaky voice that undermined the non-chalance she was attempting '—but the guards came in time.'

'You must have been terrified,' he murmured.

'And badly shaken,' she said with a nod. 'I was in such shock when they took me home that I barely heard what my mother and grandmother said.'

'Barely?'

'I wish I hadn't heard any of it,' she admitted softly. 'I was so hurt by what this boy I thought I loved—because how could it have been real?—had done but they insisted on saying *I told you so*. My mother hadn't been as in-the-know about it as my grandmother, but it didn't matter. They ripped into me, and made me regret I'd ever taken a chance like that.'

'But it wasn't only that,' he said, knowing they'd merely given Nalini a reason to believe what she'd been telling herself all along.

'Maybe not, but did it really matter? I'd done such a foolish thing. I hadn't only put myself in danger, but the Crown too. I was third in line to the throne—didn't I realise what that meant?' She sighed now. 'But they were right.'

'No, they weren't.'

She smiled. 'You don't even know what I was going to say.'

'Yes, I do.' He shoved his hands into his trouser pockets to stave off the temptation to take her into his arms again. 'You were going to say that they were right to point out that you shouldn't have left the castle. That you shouldn't have fallen for someone below your position. That you should have listened to them. That you should have obeyed.' He paused. 'It was probably very similar to what they told you when you decided to come here. Or when you told them about the wedding.'

She blinked, and then nodded. 'Okay, fine, so you do know. But I thought that they were right. Then. And every day after, I made sure that I didn't ever put myself into that position again. I did what they said, I listened. I wanted to prove that I was responsible.'

'Except with me.'

'I thought they'd eventually see that I *was* being responsible in coming here. In saving our kingdom.' She paused. 'But I think I always knew that they wouldn't.'

'So why did you come?'

'Because I was so unhappy,' she admitted. 'I did everything they wanted me to and I… I lost myself. I mean, I'd lost a part of myself on that beach.' She rolled her eyes. 'The part that believed in love and romance and happiness. I realised that for me, for us—*royalty*—those things weren't a reality. But I used to be excited about things. About painting and music and sometimes even my royal duties. And then…then I wasn't any more. I was just going through the motions of my life without living it. I may not have believed in the things I did before, but I sure as hell didn't want to just go through the motions.'

She hadn't moved from where she was in front of him when she'd pulled her hands from his, and now she laid a hand on his cheek for a brief moment before dropping it. 'You gave me a reason to *live* again. And to be excited about things. Like painting.' She bit her lip and there was hesitation in her eyes when she spoke again. 'I hadn't painted a picture like the one I did for you since that night. A painting with emotion and…and *passion*.'

Moved, he cleared his throat. 'But you painted the picture of the beach? After, I mean.'

Her eyes turned contemplative. 'Yes, you're right. But that painting wasn't for joy. It was a form of therapy. And a reminder to make better decisions. To be careful.'

He realised then why she'd been so upset when she'd seen it. 'Your grandmother sent it to you because she knew?'

'I never told her, so perhaps she didn't know exactly.' She was angry, he saw, and wondered at the fact that he could read her expressions now. Something turned in his chest. 'But she knew enough. And I knew she wanted to remind me about what happened the last time I made my own decision.'

'Unbelievable.'

'But true,' she replied mildly. 'That's why I was so determined to make things work between us. That's what it was the first day,' she continued. 'I wanted to prove to us both that my decision wasn't a mistake. If it had been—'

'It would prove what she'd been saying all along.'

'And I would go back to doubting myself.'

'Do you?' he asked softly. 'Do you still doubt yourself?'

'I don't know,' she replied in the same tone, but her eyes twinkled when she looked up at him. 'Was this a mistake?'

He smiled, and felt his heart thunder in his chest. 'I don't think so.'

'Neither do I.'

Silence beat between them, before Zacchaeus pulled his hands from his pockets and settled them lightly on her waist. 'You're not a fool. And what you told me… It isn't foolish. You had every right to feel the way you felt about it. And I know why you kept it from me.'

'Th…thank you,' she said in an unsteady voice, and then cleared her throat. 'Thank you for un-derstanding.'

'I would have,' he replied. 'I always would have understood. I wouldn't have judged you. I never will, no matter what you do.'

Her hands moved to his chest, one resting over the heart that was still thumping. 'I know. You're better than I ever imagined you would be. This was definitely not a mistake.'

His lips curved. 'So you trust me now?'

'Do you trust me?'

'More than anyone else I've ever known,' he whispered, and found that it was true.

It stunned him, but he was too caught in her eyes, in the way he could suddenly read exactly what she wanted to care.

'Me, too.' She licked her lips and the pounding of his heart rippled through his blood, creating a heady ache in his body. 'We should go back,' she told him.

But she moved closer to him.

'They'll miss us,' he replied softly.

His eyes flickered down to her lips that were still moist.

'At the very least they'll wonder where we are.'

Her hands moved from his chest to around his waist.

'And they'll make up reasons about why we didn't return.'

His thumb brushed over her lips.

'It'll cause a scandal.' Her body pressed against his. 'A husband and wife leaving their wedding reception before their guests.'

'A newly married couple.' His hands loosened

the buttons at the back of her dress. 'Sneaking off on their wedding night.'

'It's unheard of.'

She pushed his jacket from his shoulders. Started on the buttons of his shirt.

'Absolutely.'

The dress fell to the floor just as she finished opening his shirt, and he swallowed at what it revealed. 'Somehow I don't think I'll care,' he told her hoarsely.

She nodded, her eyes hot, and before she touched her lips to his, whispered, 'Me neither.'

CHAPTER SEVENTEEN

NALINI WOKE UP with the sun shining on her.

It took her a while to realise that she wasn't in the bed that had become familiar to her over the past weeks, but in Zacchaeus's. And some more time to realise why the heat of the sun had woken her.

She was lying on the side of the bed directly opposite the window.

She was also naked.

It didn't take long for the memories to return then, and she felt her body grow hot from embarrassment just as much as it did from remembering what they'd got up to the night before. She was prepared for neither. And didn't have the chance to ponder on either before realising she was alone in the bed, too.

It took longer than anticipated to convince herself that it didn't mean anything. And she had to repeat that to herself as she took her shower.

The heat of the water soothed aching muscles, sensitive flesh, and the breath shuddered from her lungs at the reason for them.

She was annoyed that she'd woken up alone. And that annoyance covered her panic at what she'd done, no matter how many times she told herself that she hadn't done anything wrong. Still, the uneasy feeling sheathed her heart, forcing her to acknowledge it with every pump.

It would go away when she saw him, she thought, as she chose her outfit for the day. There was only the briefest moment of hesitation before she picked out a bright yellow dress that would tell the world she was a happy bride who had been thoroughly ravished on her wedding night.

Well, one of those was true.

She hated that she still had doubts after what she'd shared with Zacchaeus the night before. An intimacy that she couldn't have imagined in her wildest dreams. Not only physically—she laid a hand on her chest as though it would keep her heart from reacting to the thought—but emotionally, too. She'd told him about Josh, about the beach. She'd told him about all her insecurities—had revealed that she doubted herself, her decisions.

It wasn't unusual under those circumstances to want to wake up with the person she'd opened up to. To see his face and know that she hadn't made a mistake. That the love she'd felt between them the night before hadn't only been in her head.

Love.

She'd been ready to leave the room and go down for breakfast before she'd thought that. Before she'd found that it hadn't been a realisation but an acknowledgement. The *realisation* had come the night she'd agreed to bring the wedding forward. And the process of it had started long, long before that night.

She'd been in free fall ever since.

Nalini knew now that part of the reason she hadn't wanted to tell Zacchaeus about Josh was because it would strip away that guard she'd put up to prevent herself from admitting she loved him. She'd used what she'd felt for Josh after one month as an excuse not to acknowledge the more intense feelings she'd felt for Zacchaeus in half that time.

Because somewhere in her mind she'd known that when she told Zacchaeus about Josh, the word, the emotion—*love*—that now came naturally with Zacchaeus would no longer be able to taunt her. And she hadn't been sure whether taunting would be better than knowing.

But she couldn't pretend that she didn't know now. She'd told Zacchaeus the truth, and the tumultuous feelings inside her told her she couldn't ignore the cause any more.

But the part of her that wanted to jump for joy that she loved *her husband* was silenced by the part demanding to know why he'd left her.

Because she'd learnt how intuitive Zacchaeus was the previous night. He knew exactly what to say to make her feel warm, comforted. Feelings she'd rarely—if ever—felt before she'd got to know him. He also knew exactly what to do to make her body feel things she'd never felt before, too…

She took a steadying breath and went down to breakfast.

The first thing she noticed was that Zacchaeus wasn't there. Nor were her mother and grandmother, or Alika, Spencer and the nephew she'd barely seen the night before. The only people who *were* there were Leyna and Xavier. She plastered a smile on her face when they looked over at her, and then felt it fall away as soon as she got a good look at Leyna.

'What's wrong?' She strode to the table. 'Should I call for the royal physician?'

Pale as she was, Leyna offered her a weak smile. 'That's not necessary.'

'But you look awful.'

'Nalini!' Xavier said sharply, but Leyna smiled more broadly now.

'It's fine, Xav. She's probably right.'

'No, she's not,' Xavier replied in a soft voice, shooting Nalini a thunderous look.

'He's right,' Nalini said quickly. 'I made a mistake.'

'No, you didn't,' Leyna said wryly and nibbled on a piece of dry toast. 'But, honestly, it's fine. I really don't have the energy to pretend like I care what anyone thinks about how I look.'

'So you *are* ill.'

Nalini watched as Leyna and Xavier exchanged a look, and quickly realised what it meant. Her eyes widened and a smile—wider than she'd ever thought she would give that morning—spread across her face.

'No,' Xavier said quickly when Nalini opened her mouth. 'Don't say it aloud. Not here.'

Annoyance dampened her excitement. 'The people here are perfectly trustworthy. No one will know you're a *fornicator*.' She whispered the last word, but so salaciously that even Leyna chuckled.

'Now that you're married you think you know everything, don't you,' Xavier said dryly—though was that a flush on his skin?

She smiled, but shook her head. She wasn't going to fall into that trap. 'I'm very happy for you both. How far along?'

'Early enough to have it be a honeymoon baby,' Leyna answered.

'An extremely premature one,' Xavier added, a frown furrowing his brow.

'But your invitations are out,' Nalini offered, hating to see her brother so perturbed. 'You're marrying early autumn. It's only a few more weeks away.'

It had been another reason to rush her own wedding. Not that she'd thought of it when she'd offered to bring the date forward, but it had been a good idea after all. She wouldn't want to overshadow the excitement of the wedding of the century. While hers had been merely a royal society wedding, considering that she was a princess, and her King... Well, her King wasn't entirely liked by the world at the moment.

'I'm sorry if I affected your plans in any way,' she told Leyna.

'You haven't,' came the reply. 'Besides, we're indebted to you. If you hadn't agreed to this, we might not be sitting here together, sharing this meal.'

'We don't know what will happen in the future,' Xavier said darkly. 'Macoa is still a threat.'

'Which we'll deal with if and when the time comes,' Leyna said smoothly, and Nalini felt relief flood through her. Her gaze moved between Leyna and Xavier, and envy took the place of relief, before giving way to guilt.

She shouldn't feel jealous of what Leyna and Xavier had. She should be happy that her brother was finally happy. She thought of all he'd been through—having his heart broken by Leyna when he was barely an adult, and then having to mourn the death of the wife he'd married shortly after. Her brother *deserved* the second chance he'd got with his first love.

So why was she suddenly wishing for a chance at love, too?

Just because she'd discovered she was in love with Zacchaeus didn't suddenly mean she would be unrealistic. That she would *hope*. Because though the weight of the night on the beach with Josh had been lifted somewhat, it didn't mean that she'd gone back to being the Nalini she'd been before.

But that's not entirely true.

She frowned at the inner voice and busied herself with preparing her breakfast so she didn't draw attention to herself. But she didn't think she would be able to eat the croissant she'd placed on her plate. Panic and worry were churning in her stomach, destroying her appetite.

She knew she didn't trust the Nalini she'd been before that night on the beach but… But hadn't she told Zacchaeus just the night before that she'd *wanted* to be the person she'd been before that night? That she wanted her will to live back—that she wanted to be excited, to be *happy* about life again?

The uncertainty of it turned in her mind and she sipped her coffee, hoping the caffeine would offer her mind some clarity. She gave it a few minutes, and sighed in relief when it seemed to work.

Yes, she'd wanted to live life again, but that wouldn't make her naïve. Just because she wanted to be happy, excited, didn't mean she wanted to go back to making mistakes. She just wanted to believe in herself again. To stop trying to change the way her family saw her. To claim back the self-belief and confidence that night—and her grandmother and mother's reaction to it—had robbed her of.

And it had worked somewhat, she thought, re-membering Xavier's words to her the night before. Her brother no longer seemed to think of her as the reckless teenager he'd warned to be careful before she'd come to Kirtida. And since she knew her grandmother and mother wouldn't be changing their minds—not when they didn't seem to want to—she told herself that that would be enough.

To prove it, she asked Xavier about her family members' absence.

'Did Mama leave?'

'Early this morning,' Xavier confirmed, apology flashing in his eyes. 'They'll get over it, Lini.'

'Like they got over the whole Josh thing?' Nalini said lightly, and told herself it would take time for the wounds to heal. 'Alika?'

'They left with Mama. I don't think they had a choice, but Alika asked me to tell you they were sorry and that she'd call you later today.'

Nalini nodded, and forced the emotion from her voice. 'And Zacchaeus? Have you seen him this morning?'

'We haven't.' Xavier frowned. 'Did you two not sort things out last night? When you didn't come back last night we all assumed—'

'No, we're fine,' Nalini interrupted her brother, her face burning. She didn't care what he'd assumed—he was still her brother. And she could live her entire life without knowing that he knew what she'd done on the night of her wedding. 'He must be out for his morning run.'

Nalini had no idea whether that was true, but

she wasn't going to admit that her husband had slipped out of bed that morning to avoid her.

You don't know if that's true, the voice in her mind supplied, but she ignored it. 'When are you two leaving?'

'We were supposed to be gone a while ago already, but Leyna wasn't quite feeling up to it.'

'I'm better now,' she piped up, the dry piece of toast half-eaten and the colour back in her face. 'We should probably leave before that changes.'

Nalini saw them off and, as she waved, felt both relieved and anxious about being without them on Kirtida. Relieved because she knew her brother saw too much. When he'd kissed her goodbye, he'd given her a long, hard look that had her blushing and looking away. But he'd only murmured that she should look after herself—Leyna's work once again, Nalini thought.

And now that they were gone, along with all the other guests who'd come for the wedding, she was forced to face the fact that she was alone. The fact that she would have a completely new life on Kirtida. There was no more ignoring it. She was now a queen, and would be for the rest of her life. She'd disrupted her entire world because of it, and now she'd be living the reality of it.

But, in a more immediate sense, Nalini was alone because her husband had abandoned her. She rolled her eyes at the thought, and as she set out to find him, hoped she was just being dramatic.

'Oh, you're alive,' Nalini greeted him when he walked into the bedroom.

Emotion tumbled through him when he saw her. She was wearing a bright yellow dress, a stark contrast to the darkness of the night clear in the windows behind her chair. The last time he'd seen her, she'd been completely naked, sleeping in his bed. Beguiling, beautiful, and so very tempting.

He'd had to escape as soon as he could.

'I had matters to attend to.'

'Me too,' Nalini replied. 'I had to see off the last of our guests.'

'Only your family remained.'

'They were guests,' she repeated, her voice tight. 'I also had the pleasure of lying to them about where you were.'

'I'll send them a note to apologise.'

She laughed mockingly. 'Yes, do that.' When she stood, her dress fell to her knees, drawing his attention to her legs. Legs that had been wrapped around him the night before…

'And now that I know you weren't in some kind of danger, I'll leave you to write your note.'

She tried to walk past him, but he stopped her by sliding a hand around her waist. 'That's what you thought? That I was in danger?'

'How was I supposed to know?' she snapped. 'You just *left*. I didn't know what to think, and danger was preferable to the other thoughts I had, quite frankly.'

'What did you think?' he asked quietly.

'Well, we got married yesterday and then I told you about the most defining experience of my life and we made love.' He winced at her bluntness. 'So, thinking about you in danger was better than thinking you'd run away from me.'

His arm dropped to his side. 'I wasn't running.'

'Of course not. It's not like you've run away from everything that's forced you out of your comfort zone.'

'What's that supposed to mean?'

'I've just noticed a pattern, Zacchaeus. Like this whole thing with Macoa. Instead of turning to your allies for help, you waited *weeks* before saying anything. And the only reason you did was because they'd forced your hand.'

'You know why—'

'And then there's your parents. Have you ever dealt with the way their actions have affected your life? Or have you just been going along with it, ignoring it day after day, *running*?'

'You don't know what you're talking about,' he growled, and resisted the prickling in his chest at her words.

'Maybe not. But I'm not running.'

'You haven't been running away from what you told me last night?'

Her eyes flashed. 'The second part of your sentence contradicts the first. Try again.'

'Do you want to talk about last night, Nalini?' He stepped closer to her, feeling the anger radiate off him. 'Do you want to talk about how we kissed, how we touched, how I took your—'

'Don't.' The word was said fiercely, sharply, with so much emotion that it shut him up. 'I don't care what's happening with you today, Zacchaeus, but you will *not* take what happened between us last night and turn it into something dirty.'

Hurt—pure and simple—settled on her face. He didn't think he'd ever feel as bad as he did right in that moment. But when she spoke again he realised he was wrong.

'I know it meant something to you. So much that you felt the need to disappear for our entire first day of being married to deal with it.' She paused. 'Unless I'm wrong? Did something happen with your father? Macoa?'

Shame had the words sticking in his throat, and he shook his head. She gave one quick nod.

'Right, so you were running.' There was another pause. 'Goodnight, Zacchaeus.'

She walked out of the room and, though he urged his legs to move, to go after her, they remained where they were. It was a long time before they did move, and then it was to his shower and not after his wife.

Why did he keep thinking of her that way? It was as if a switch had been flicked, and suddenly he couldn't think of her as anything other than his wife. The woman who would rule by his side. Who would bear his children. Who would ensure that he was no longer alone.

He threw off his clothes and put the shower on full pressure, hoping to drown his thoughts. But they stayed with him. Just as they had during the hours he'd spent aimlessly driving around his kingdom, looking for answers he hadn't found until he'd come home and spoken to Nalini.

He'd been running.

He'd been running from the emotion that had nearly choked him when he'd looked down at Nalini in his arms, her face still flushed from their love-making, but so sleepy she could barely keep her eyes open. He'd been running from the tenderness that he'd felt brushing the curls from her face, from pressing a kiss against those soft, full lips. And the complete and utter infatuation he'd felt when she'd given him a sleepy smile and snuggled into him, her heart beating rhythmically, steadily, against his own.

For the first time in his life he hadn't felt alone. And it was that, and the fact that she was his *wife*, and the feelings thrumming through his blood—feelings that had finally caught up with him—that had prompted him to slip out of the room as soon as the sun had come up and drive around the whole of his kingdom.

He'd known it would hurt her. Had hated himself *for* hurting her. But he knew he would have made it worse if he'd stayed and she'd woken up to him that morning. If she'd looked at him with that warmth in her eyes and that complete and utter trust. No, her anger was better. He could handle that. He could even handle her disappointment. In fact, he welcomed it.

Weren't those *supposed* to be the feelings of a wife, after all?

He let the water run over his head for a few more minutes and then got out of the shower, dressed and poured himself a drink. If he was honest with himself, he knew that that had disintegrated the box he'd hidden his feelings in.

Thinking about his mother. Witnessing her be a wife to his father. And a terrible one at that.

He knew that being honest with himself would send him down a rabbit hole he would struggle to climb out of again. He'd been keeping himself above it for most of the day—running from it, as Nalini said. But now that he'd thought it, he realised it was too late. It was sucking him in, forcing him to think about his parents.

About all the times he'd seen them argue. About how his mother had blamed his father for things that had never been Jaydon's fault. He remembered the countless instances he'd told himself that he'd never want what they had. That he would never want a political marriage.

And now that he had one, what did that mean?

No matter how long, how hard he thought about it, he couldn't come up with an answer. But he knew someone who could help him figure it out. So he set his drink, still full, aside and prepared to have a long, honest conversation with his father.

CHAPTER EIGHTEEN

SHE WANTED TO PAINT. She also wanted to be outside in the garden.

But she didn't want to paint outside and lose the privacy she had indoors. And since her need to be out in the open, away from the confines of the castle—which were beginning to suffocate her—trumped her desire to release her emotions onto a canvas, she opted for a walk in the garden.

Nalini took a deep breath as she made her way through the trees, following along the stream she'd fallen into at their engagement shoot. Where they'd shared their first kiss that same night. Her life had been significantly less complicated then, she thought. And laughed when she realised she'd thought her life complicated *then*.

But she gave herself the benefit of the doubt, and blamed it on inexperience. It was different from how she'd dealt with her mistakes before. When everything with Josh had happened, she'd hated that she'd been so inexperienced. Naïve. Irresponsible.

But now she knew that she deserved more than to think of herself that way. She knew that it was enough to know that she'd changed. And she felt so sure about all of it that she refused to consider what her inexperience had cost her this time around.

Though she could hardly ignore it.

The pain of her broken heart was there in every breath, in every movement. The panic that she'd got it all wrong was still lingering in her mind. But she didn't want to live like that any more. She'd left Mattan because she wanted to get away from the person she'd become. That person had been unkind to herself. She'd been so terrified of making mistakes—of living up, or down, rather, to the expectations her family had of her—that she didn't trust that she had learnt. That she had grown.

It had taken an entire week to come to that conclusion. And now that she had she finally felt a sense of the freedom she'd so intensely longed for. *And* the independence she'd wanted, considering she'd been relying on herself for the past week since her husband had seemingly disappeared...

And, yes, maybe she had spent the first half of the week weeping about a relationship that had never existed. She wasn't sure how she'd convinced herself that she was in a relationship—personal, not political—with Zacchaeus. Perhaps it had been sleeping together...

But as soon as that thought had occurred to her she'd dismissed it. She'd thought there was something more between them long before their wedding night. That was the very reason she'd slept with him that night after all.

It had panicked her, but then she'd realised that it wasn't the same as with her and Josh. Because *she* wasn't the same. And that was the difference, she'd realised. She could be terrified that she'd made a mistake coming to Kirtida, marrying Zacchaeus. She could be *petrified* that she'd fallen in love with him.

Or she could accept that it had happened and move forward.

There was plenty else to focus on. She was

Queen now. She had a new home to explore and relationships, friendships, to develop. She'd rediscovered her love of painting, and would seek solace in that instead of in the arms of her husband. She would be fine, she told herself over the voice in her head telling her it wouldn't be that easy.

It might not be easy but it would be worth it, she thought, and settled at the bank of the stream, pulling her shoes off to dip her feet into the water.

'Careful. We wouldn't want you falling in.'

Her hair stood on end at Zacchaeus's voice, and the zen she'd felt abruptly disappeared as she heard him settle down next to her. Stubbornly, she refused to look at him. Or to acknowledge him at all. She closed her eyes and took another deep breath, willing herself to focus on how the breeze felt a little cooler today. The first sign of autumn coming, she thought.

But no matter how much she wanted to focus on the weather, she couldn't. Because every time she took a breath she smelled that knee-weakening scent of his. It had her opening her eyes, clenching her jaw, before she managed to grind out, 'What do you want?'

'I thought I'd spend the afternoon with my wife.'

'Too little, too late. I have no intention of—'

'You didn't let me finish,' he interrupted her quietly. 'I thought we could talk.'

'I don't want to talk.'

'Why not?'

'Because I don't want to keep feeling this way. After every conversation we have I feel awful, and it takes me so long to right myself again.' She refused to look at him. 'I'm fine with the way things are. With not seeing each other. I'm fine with you running. I just don't want to keep running with you.'

'I'm not running any more.'

That got her attention and when she looked at him she wished she'd kept to her resolve. Because now she couldn't get the image of him with that wounded look out of her mind long enough to find the strength to leave him at the stream.

'What happened?'

'My father...' Zacchaeus's face paled. 'I think

I've… I've finally allowed myself to face the fact that he's dying.'

She reached out, squeezed his hand, and then snatched it back. 'I'm sorry.'

He nodded and there was a long pause before he spoke again. 'I don't want him to die.'

'Of course you don't. He's your father.'

'I don't want him to die,' Zacchaeus said again, almost as if he hadn't heard her, 'when I'm so damn angry at him.'

The anger heated his skin so much that Zacchaeus wished he could take off his clothes and let the stream run over him. But he knew that would only give him temporary relief. He'd tried having a cold shower after every single visit with his father, since that first night he'd decided to speak with him.

But Zacchaeus's first reaction that night had been to face the pain. His father was dying, and Nalini had been right about how he'd dealt with it—he hadn't.

He'd ignored the reality of what his father's illness meant, had instead focused on protecting Kirtida. But now that that was no longer such a pressing factor, he couldn't keep ignoring that the man he loved and respected would be leaving him soon.

During that first meeting with his father he'd been overwhelmed with emotion. Zacchaeus hadn't been able to ask the questions he'd needed to. He'd spent his time telling his father about the wedding, about the alliance. He'd basically spent all that time telling his father he didn't have to worry about the future of Kirtida any more. Zacchaeus had stayed the night at his father's side, afraid that that peace of mind would finally be a reason for his father to let go.

But when he'd woken up the next morning, his father had seemed better, stronger than the day before. And Zacchaeus had realised he needed to ask his questions now, before it was too late.

After that conversation, the heat—the *anger*—had begun, and when he'd returned to his room he'd taken an ice-cold shower. But that had only helped to cool his skin and as soon as he'd finished he'd felt the heat all over again.

And so it had gone for the last week. Somehow Zacchaeus had found himself caught between his anger and love for his father. Between not wanting to see Jaydon again and being unable to stop himself from spending hours there. Just because Jaydon was feeling better again didn't mean he was miraculously healed. In fact, the royal physician had warned that it could mean the exact opposite.

Zacchaeus would never be able to forgive himself if he let his anger—or any of the other emotions he was feeling—keep him from his father. Especially during what could be his last days.

But it was hard on Zacchaeus, and he'd spent hours in silence at his father's side some days. Others, he couldn't stop the questions from pouring out of his lips. His father would answer what he could—or what he chose to.

And Zacchaeus had found it all so dark, so overwhelming, until he couldn't take it any more and had to find his source of light.

Even though he hadn't seen her in almost seven full days.

'You're angry at him?' Nalini asked. 'For dying?'

'No.' Then he thought about it, and realised there was truth in that, too. 'Yes, maybe I am.'

'That's normal,' she said soothingly. But she didn't touch him again, even though he saw her curl her fingers into a fist as if she'd wanted to. 'I felt the same way after my father died.'

'Does it ever go away?'

She didn't answer him immediately. 'I think that first burst of anger does. The completely irrational kind. You realise that it isn't their fault—that they didn't intentionally choose to leave.' She paused. 'But… It's still hard at times. You miss them, and it's easier to blame them for their absence than to face the pain of it. I imagine it must be the same with an illness.'

'More, maybe. Because they're not gone yet and now you know…you *know* that they will be and you have to say everything you want to say to them. But you can't. There's no time and you're…you're stuck,' he ended helplessly, unsure of where all those words had come from.

'You don't have to feel bad about it,' she said softly. 'Don't feel bad for your feelings, whatever they are.'

'But I do.'

'Why?'

'Because *they* are bad.'

'You mean…negative?'

He nodded now, unable to put it into words any more.

'That's fine too. I doubt there's a child out there who doesn't have negative feelings towards their parents.'

'Has your mother been…?' He faltered.

Could he ask about how her mother had been since their wedding? He would have known, after all, if he'd been there. If he'd been an actual husband. Guilt added to the heat.

'Oh, she's been…' Nalini shrugged. 'I haven't spoken to her since the wedding. I figured I'd give her some time to adjust to this new reality.'

'I'm sorry.'

'Don't apologise. It's not like it's your fault.' There was a beat of silence and then she giggled. It was a sound he hadn't expected to hear from her that day, but one he'd desperately needed to. 'Actually, all of this *is* kind of your fault.'

And for the first time in a week he felt his lips curve. 'I'm not sure that's entirely fair.'

Her smile faded and she tilted her head. 'Things aren't always fair.'

He realised then that he hadn't been treating *her* very fairly and told himself to swallow his pride. 'I know I'm a part of the reason you're saying that and… Well, I'm sorry.'

'What are you apologising for, Zacchaeus?'

'For…for not being around this last week.'

'That's it?'

He opened his mouth, but realised that the question was a trap. If he said yes, she would surely tell him all the things that he had to be sorry for. If he said no, she would expect him to elaborate and he wouldn't be able to.

His mind raced through the possibilities, and settled on what she'd said when he'd joined her. That is was too late to spend time with her. But wasn't that what he'd just apologised for? There was more, he thought, and remembered that she'd also said she needed to recover from their conversations. What did that mean?

Before he could ask, she shook her head. 'You know what, you don't have to answer that. Your silence has already answered my question.'

'Now *you're* not being fair,' he said. 'Regardless of what answer I'd have given you, it would have been the wrong one. And now you're telling me that *no answer* was wrong too?'

'Why are you here, Zacchaeus?' she asked

again. 'And I don't want any of that "wanting to spend time with me" crap.'

'It's not crap. I really wanted to spend time with you.'

'Why?'

'That's a stupid question.'

'Not as stupid as you being unable to answer me.' She waited, and then gave a bark of laughter. 'I can't believe this.' She slipped her wet feet into her shoes and pushed up from the ground, refusing the help he offered her as soon as he'd realised her intention and stood.

'Nalini, come on. I just wanted to spend some time with you. I've been with my father basically every moment since we last spoke. I need some…some reprieve from that.'

'And what would you like me to do to help? Sing a song? Tell a joke?'

He felt the anger ripple again. 'You know that's not what I mean.'

'Well, you can't seem to tell me what you mean, so how am I supposed to know?' She didn't wait for an answer. 'I'm fine with you leaving me to deal with the aftermath of the wedding, to write thank you notes and call to make sure our guests arrived home safely. I'm fine with you disappearing after we *made love* and ignoring the fact that I'm a human being. With feelings. And that I'd have feelings about the fact that *we made love*.' Scarlet streaked across her cheeks. 'But I'm *not* fine with you using me whenever *you* think it's an appropriate time.'

She took a step closer to him and poked him in the chest. 'Because, regardless of what you think, I *am* a human being and I *do* have feelings. I'm not going to accept being treated like this again.'

She stomped off, leaving him speechless. And when his thoughts had finally caught up with his lips, he opened his mouth to tell her that that was absolutely ridiculous. But she was gone.

He ran back to the castle and asked the first person he saw where Nalini was. Though the man didn't know where she'd been heading, Zacchaeus had a fairly good idea. An idea that was confirmed when he reached the tower room and saw her pacing there.

The room had more paintings in it now, and his eyes flew over them before he spoke. There were paintings of the storm on the beach the night of their date, and of the room next to the kitchen where they'd spent that evening. There was a painting of the church they'd been married in, and of the hall where they'd held their reception.

But there were also paintings of him. One that perfectly captured the way he'd felt when he'd seen her on their wedding day, and the way he'd looked at her during their first dance. There was only one of them together—they were in each other's arms, staring intently into each other's eyes. He recognised it as the moment before they'd made love, and when his eyes finally met hers again he realised what she'd been asking him to apologise for.

'I'm so sorry, Nalini.'

'You've already said that.'

'But now I know... I've hurt you and I'm sorry.'

'I've been hurt before,' she said softly, and her expression told him that she meant him to think that it was no big deal. But he knew that it was, and the fact that she was comparing him to the jerk who'd hurt her so long ago confirmed it.

'But I shouldn't have been the one to hurt you.'

'Spouses hurt each other all the time.'

'You're right. But those who want a healthy relationship should apologise. They shouldn't let it build and build until there's nothing left in the marriage except a piece of paper binding it.'

Her expression softened. 'You're right. But you're not talking about us, are you?'

'No, I am,' he disagreed. 'Just as it should be. Us. You and me.' He blew out a breath, felt his shoulders tighten. 'I've been letting my parents get between us from the moment you arrived at Kirtida. I won't let that happen any more.'

CHAPTER NINETEEN

'THOUGH PERHAPS I should thank them,' Zacchaeus continued. 'They *are* the reason you're on Kirtida, after all.'

Nalini let the attempt at lightening the mood float over her and instead focused on the hurt she saw clear in Zacchaeus's eyes. He was trying to pretend that the realisation he'd just come to hadn't affected him. He was trying to shrug it off, to make it seem unimportant.

But she knew him well enough now to recognise when he was pretending. Hadn't she known from the moment she'd arrived on Kirtida that he wasn't the man he was pretending to be?

And suddenly everything changed for her. All the excuses, the front that she would be fine without him. She only had to look around the room at her paintings to realise that she'd only been fooling herself.

She only had to look at the man in front of

her to realise that her love for him wouldn't be ignored.

'They hurt you.'

His eyes met hers and she hoped he would see what she wanted to say in her own. That he didn't have to keep up a front any more. That he didn't have to be alone. She was there, and he could trust her with everything whirling around in his mind. He could lean on her—he would always be able to.

'Yes,' he said, seemingly getting her message. 'I only realised how much the day after our wedding. After you fell asleep in my arms the night before, actually.'

'You were afraid I'd hurt you like they did?'

'I… I couldn't put into words how I felt,' he said a little helplessly. 'All I knew was that I was completely overwhelmed with emotions I couldn't name and so I… I left that morning to try and figure out what they were.'

'Did you?'

'Not then. But when I came back, after I spoke to you…' His lips twisted into a wry smile. 'I *had* been running from everything that I'd been feeling. I knew it, but that didn't keep me from running. But after speaking to you… I figured I'd talk to my father, because I knew some of it came from my mother. From the fact that their marriage was so messed up. And now that I was married—'

'You were scared it would somehow be the same for you.'

'Yes.' He ran a hand over the back of his neck. 'And I think I was afraid that you'd hurt me, too. Because you'd started to mean something to me, and the only other people I'd cared for… They'd betrayed that trust I gave them.'

Her heart filled, but she forced herself to calm down. This wasn't about whether he cared for her. It was about getting him to be okay with the fact that he did.

'How?'

'It's…complicated. And I'm not saying that because I don't want you to know,' he added with a smile—a nod to their previous conversations. 'I'm saying it because… Well, there are so many feelings. I think they both betrayed me by being such terrible parents. As close to my dad as I was growing up, I can see that he wasn't a good father now. He was a fair one, and an excellent mentor, but not a father. And my mother?' He gave a menacing laugh. 'She wasn't a mother at all. I had no relationship with her. Still don't. But I expected her to stay. To be a queen. To be a family.'

His eyes met hers. 'We were a messed-up family, but it was the only one I knew. And her leaving, and all the stuff that happened afterwards, with Macoa? She broke the unspoken rules of our family.'

'Do you have any idea…why she left?'

'No. But I hate that she did, and that she left such a mess. And I hate that my father asked me to go along with his plan—with the coup—because he didn't want *her* to know he was ill. I feel like I'm a pawn. And now that my father can no longer play, he wants me to take over for him.'

Surprise clutched her heart. 'He asked you to do that?'

'Not directly. But what do you think this coup was?' He began to pace. 'And then I had to pull strings to protect the kingdom. The *kingdom*. They were both supposed to protect it, but instead they put their people in danger. All because of their hatred for each other.'

No wonder he was turned inside out, she thought, and let go of all the resentment she felt about the last week. '*You* protected them, though. They're your people now, and you protected them.'

'But what happens if my mother chooses to go ahead with this plan?' His tone was desperate. 'I wish she would just wait. Just until...' He stopped pacing and braced his hands on his knees. She nearly stepped forward, but he straightened again and she waited for the words that had caused him such anguish. 'Just until my father goes,' he continued in a strangled voice.

Seconds passed before either of them spoke.

'You could ask her,' Nalini suggested softly.

'What? Ask the woman who left her family to live with her lover for *compassion*?'

'People are rarely as bad as their actions make them seem,' she replied, and her thoughts turned to her own family. Perhaps it was time she had an honest conversation with her mother and grandmother, she thought, and then brushed it away. 'It's only a suggestion, and if she says yes...'

She let the possibility linger, and saw that he was considering it. But his eyes changed suddenly when he looked at her, and her heart started to thud.

'What?'

'You're amazing.'

'No, I'm just trying to help.'

'I don't deserve your help.'

'You're my husband.'

'And that means something to you, doesn't it?' He was staring at her intensely and she felt her cheeks grow hot.

'I'm not sure what you mean.'

'I mean that this isn't only some political thing for you. You…you actually believe in marriage.'

She laughed softly. 'I didn't want to. I convinced myself that I didn't, in fact. For a very long time.'

'Because of Josh?' She nodded. 'What changed your mind?'

'You.'

He wasn't sure why the answer surprised him so much. Perhaps because there was still a part of him that was tainted by witnessing his parents' marriage.

But something told him that was about to change.

'What about me?' he asked softly, and breached the gap between them.

'Well, you…' He loved the colour of her cheeks—how, when she was feeling uncertain, she pulled at a curl. 'You…you showed me that I could trust you.'

'No, I didn't.' And it shamed him. 'I probably showed you the opposite when I left you in bed that morning.'

'You're not perfect,' she allowed with a small smile. 'But I understand now. You were scared.'

'You didn't have to understand. You could have been resentful. Angry.'

As he said the words, he thought *he* was beginning to understand what had happened with his parents. His father had told him that their political relationship had turned into love, but that feeling had gone away soon after they'd got married. By the time Zacchaeus had been born, their relationship had been broken.

It hadn't been anything specific, Jaydon had

told him, but numerous small things. Resentment had been conceived, anger born, and soon they were living separate lives.

But, throughout it all, Zacchaeus had realised one thing. His father still loved his mother. But his pride, his stubbornness, his hurt, had kept him from telling her that. And now her actions pierced more sharply than Jaydon would ever understand.

He would not inherit his father's foolishness.

'I've *been* angry. *And* resentful,' Nalini answered him. 'But that gave me a life I didn't want. It had me trying to prove to my family that I was someone I already was instead of trusting that *I* knew it. So I forgive you, Zacchaeus.'

'Just like that?'

'No,' she replied, just as he'd hoped she would. 'I'd like to ask you not to shut me out again. I know that you're used to being alone, but—'

'It's not that,' he interrupted. 'Or not only that. I was…scared.'

'Of what?'

'My feelings for you.' He walked towards her, stopping only a few centimetres away. 'I've seen the kind of marriage my parents had. It was a political one, just like this, and it was terrible.'

She frowned. 'You were afraid the same thing would happen to you?'

'Yes.' He leaned his forehead against hers for a moment and then drew back. 'But it won't be terrible, will it?'

'Not if we treat each other with respect. If we talk about things, and don't shut each other out.'

'I agree. But I'm not sure this marriage is strictly political any more.'

Her tongue slid over her lips and his heart began to race. If he remembered correctly, that very thing had got them into trouble the first time…

'I don't think so, no,' she whispered, and when she looked up he saw everything he needed to in her eyes.

'We've been fighting it.'

'*You've* been fighting it,' she said with a smile and wrapped her arms around his waist, resting her head on his chest. 'I've just been trying to figure out how to get it through your stubborn skull.'

'Is that any way to talk to your husband?'

he said softly, his own arms drawing her in, squeezing.

'Depends. Am I talking to him as man or king?'

He chuckled. 'They're still the same. Except, I think, they're both a little better for loving you, my queen.'

She lifted her head, her eyes shining. 'Loving?'

'Did you think I spent our wedding night with you for the sake of an heir?' he teased, and grew sober when a blush stained her cheeks. 'You did? Nalini, that's my fault. I'm sorry.'

'The thought crossed my mind. But only because I didn't want to consider that you loved me...' She trailed off and bit her lip.

He smiled. 'You don't have to be ashamed to say it. I *do* love you. And I hope you'll let me make up for the way I behaved last week.'

'Was that ever *not* an option?' she asked with a half-smile. She brushed her thumb across his cheek, and then over his lips, before laying her own there. 'I love you, too,' she whispered when she pulled back. 'And I trust you. I never thought either would be possible again.'

He tightened his arms around her. 'I still hate that you had to go through that.'

'It brought me here, to you, didn't it?' She tilted her head. 'If you have to thank your parents, then I guess I have to thank Josh—my mother, my grandmother—all of them, too.'

'Because they're the reason we're together.'

She nodded. 'But *we're* the reason we'll stay together.'

'For ever,' he promised, and kissed her again.

EPILOGUE

'AND?' NALINI ASKED as soon as Zacchaeus emerged from his library. But she didn't have to hear his answer to know what it would be. The grim, stressed lines across his forehead had eased, and the smile on his face wasn't forced.

But still she let him answer so that she could hear his success out loud. 'She agreed. My mother won't push for the divorce, and there'll be no more threats from Macoa.'

She flew into his arms and laughed when he spun her around and planted a kiss on her lips.

'Everything's going to be okay.'

'Everything's going to be okay,' she repeated, and welcomed her own relief.

She knew that for Zacchaeus, this was about more than just his mother agreeing to his suggestion. It was about speaking to his mother at all, andasking her for something. She was surprised Michelle had agreed but, just as she'd told him, Nalini believed that people were rarely as bad as they seemed.

It was also about giving his father the chance to die with dignity. About protecting his kingdom and now, she knew, protecting Mattan too.

'I can't believe it's going to be okay, that it's all over.' She gave him the time he needed to comprehend it. 'Now we can finally enjoy being married.'

'Have you not been enjoying our marriage?' she asked. 'Because I could have *sworn* you were incredibly happy last night when—'

'Ha,' he said, nuzzling her neck. 'You've become quite the comedian, haven't you?'

'Actually, I think I've always been one. You just haven't really appreciated me.'

She laughed when the nuzzle turned into a nip.

'Now I get to spend the rest of my life appreciating you. Aren't I lucky?' he said wryly, but gave her a smile that told her he thought he was. 'Do you think we should tell Leyna and Xavier? They could still stop their marriage if they wanted to.'

'Why would they want to do that?'

'Because they were forced to marry because of me.'

'You do know that they've been in love for ever?'

'I... Yes.'

'And didn't you take the credit for bringing them together?'

He grimaced. 'It was a power move. I didn't really mean it.'

She grinned. 'Yes, well, I'm sure they're grateful. Now.'

Zacchaeus tilted his head. 'So I'm kind of responsible for the happiness of the entire Isles?'

'I wouldn't go that far, mister.' She poked him in the stomach. 'I can think of at least two people who you've made very *unhappy*.'

He sobered. 'Did either your mother or grandmother take your call today?'

'No, but I know they will eventually.' She'd told herself there was nothing she could do about them not wanting to speak to her. And she reminded herself that it wouldn't last for ever. As misguided as they were, her grandmother and mother loved her. And some day they would see what she'd done for her kingdom and change their minds about who they thought she was. 'Besides, if they don't want to speak over the phone, I'll just pitch on the island. It's not like they can refuse to see me—'

She broke off when Zacchaeus picked her up and threw her over his shoulder. Pretty much like a sack of potatoes.

'Hey!'

'I know that was a jab at me.'

'No! I completely forgot you refused to see Xavier and Leyna when they tried to contact you about the alliance after you became King.'

'Really?' he asked sarcastically. 'You seem to remember the details of it quite clearly now.'

'My memory is better when I'm upside down.' He laughed, and she tapped his butt. 'Put me down.'

He immediately set her on her feet, and she frowned. 'I thought I was going to have to fight for that.'

'I was being silly anyway.' He kissed her nose. 'Come on, let's take a walk on the beach.'

She took the hand he offered and happily let him guide her to the beach. She loved this new life. She'd only been living it fully for two days, but she loved it. She loved the banter with her new husband, and how much easier he'd been to live with—how laid-back he'd become. Because she knew he was finally allowing himself the freedom, the happiness, he hadn't thought would be his.

And, yes, perhaps it was also because she was doing the same. That finally she didn't feel careless—or like a failure—because this decision had worked out. And because she knew that even if it hadn't she still would have been okay.

Waking up next to her incredibly sexy husband every day was an added benefit.

'Last time we tried this it failed horribly,' Zacchaeus said, interrupting her thoughts. She only realised then that they'd stopped a short distance from the rock they'd had their date on a while ago.

'I'm not sure *failed* is the right word.'

'Maybe not,' he replied with a smile. 'But I still thought it would be nice to try it again.'

'A little different now during the daytime,' she said softly, and let him lift her when they reached the rock. The table was set beautifully, with delicious food almost spilling over their plates and their glasses filled with champagne.

'It won't be daytime for long,' he told her.

'Sunset's coming up, and this pretty much gives you the best view of it on the island.'

'And we won't get wet?' she teased.

'We'll leave before it even becomes a possibility,' he replied, and reached into a bag she hadn't seen next to his seat. He pulled out a small square that was wrapped, and when she took it from him she felt the hollow middle that told her it was a canvas.

'What is this?'

'Open it.'

She tore the wrapping open with shaky fingers, and saw a collage of words that had been printed onto it.

'I'm not a painter,' he told her, and she heard the nerves in his voice. 'There would be no chance of me ever being able to create anything as beautiful as the portrait you made of me. But...' He took a breath. 'But I thought that I could still show you what I thought of you. I had all the words I could think of that best described you printed on it.'

Her eyes moved over the words. She knew that she wouldn't be able to read them all then, but she saw enough of them to feel the tears in her eyes. *Strong. Kind. Independent. Sweet.* And then there were the ones that he'd made up. *Kicks-you-in-the-butt-when-you-need-it. Best-kisser. Purest-heart-in-the-world.*

She bit her lip and looked up at him, and saw the anxiety in his eyes before he even asked, 'Do you like it?'

'I love it,' she whispered, and leaned over to kiss him.

'You don't have to say that,' he told her when she settled back again.

She looked at the words again, felt her heart fill as she saw new ones. 'I'm not just saying it. I love it. You know how...' Her voice wobbled and she rolled her eyes with a smile. 'You know I've never really heard any of this before.'

'That's why I wanted to do it,' he said softly. 'I just wanted you to have something that showed you how I see you. Just like your painting did for me.'

'I'm so lucky,' she said, setting the canvas on her lap. She reached for his hand and threaded her fingers through his.

'No, I'm the lucky one. You've changed me.'

His hand tightened around hers. 'You've given me the courage to be myself. To trust. To love.'

'You've done exactly the same for me. And you've given me the push I needed to believe in myself. To trust that I know who I am, and to believe that that's all that matters.'

'We're a pretty amazing couple, aren't we?'

She laughed. 'Yes, I'd say that we are.'

She sighed in contentment and settled back to watch the sun set with her husband.

* * * * *

LET'S TALK
Romance

For exclusive extracts, competitions and special offers, find us online:

f facebook.com/millsandboon

○ @millsandboonuk

𝕏 @millsandboon

Or get in touch on 0844 844 1351*

For all the latest titles coming soon, visit millsandboon.co.uk/nextmonth

*Calls cost 7p per minute plus your phone company's price per minute access charge